Sky Over El Nido

Winner of the Flannery O'Connor
Award for Short Fiction

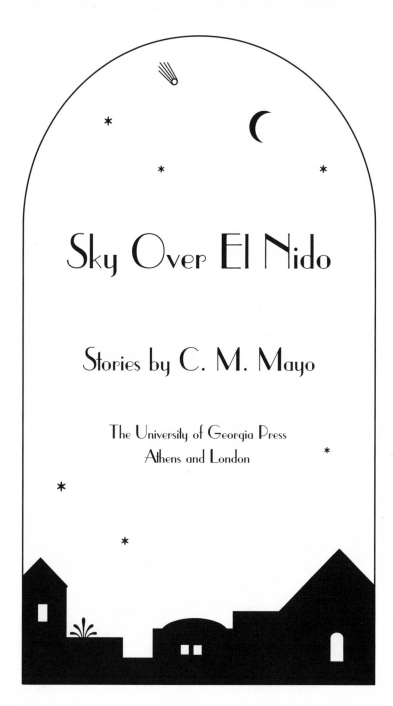

Sky Over El Nido

Stories by C. M. Mayo

The University of Georgia Press
Athens and London

*The characters in these stories are fictitious. Any resemblance to real persons,
living or dead, is unintended and entirely coincidental.*

Published by the University of Georgia Press
Athens, Georgia 30602
© 1995 by C. M. Mayo
All rights reserved
Designed by Erin Kirk New
Set in Fournier by Tseng Information Systems, Inc.
Printed and bound by Thomson-Shore, Inc.
The paper in this book meets the guidelines for permanence
and durability of the Committee on Production Guidelines
for Book Longevity of the Council on Library Resources.

Printed in the United States of America

99 98 97 96 95   C   5 4 3 2 1

Library of Congress Cataloging in Publication Data

Mayo, C. M.
Sky over El Nido : stories / by C. M. Mayo.
p.   cm.
ISBN 0-8203-1766-7
I. Title.
PS3563.A96389S59   1995
813'.54—dc20   95-9961

British Library Cataloging in Publication Data available

Two of these stories first appeared in the following
publications: "Chabela del Río y de la Fuente Contreras, Thrice
Married (Once Divorced), Reflects on Her Relationship with
Her Mother While Lying on Her Bed, Mexico City, 1990" in the
Paris Review and "The Wedding" in the *Southwest Review.*

The author gratefully acknowledges the support of the MacDowell Colony.

The story "Rainbow's End" contains a parody of "You're the Top"
by Cole Porter. Copyright © Warner/Chappell
Music, Inc.

This book is dedicated to the
memory of my grandfather

Frank R. Mayo

1908-1987

who knew how to

travel the world

*

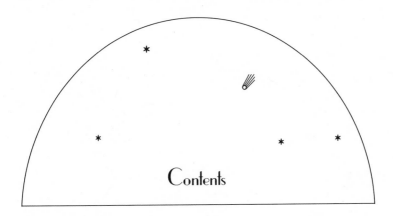

Contents

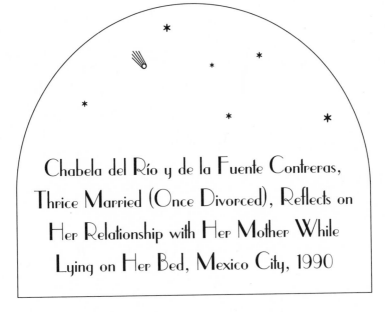

Chabela del Río y de la Fuente Contreras, Thrice Married (Once Divorced), Reflects on Her Relationship with Her Mother While Lying on Her Bed, Mexico City, 1990

Mother rescued the three zebras that escaped from the London zoo. For years, I didn't believe it.

When I was really little, she would tell me the Luftwaffe's bombs were as loud as a sweet potato man's steamer, like a jet engine on the runway. When I was a year or so older, she let me know that the bombs were far-off whistles, exploding out in the suburbs. Then, when I was too old to be bounced on her knee, she said the bombs were hitting the flats next door, the bandstand in the park, the bridge over the Thames. One flattened the neighbor's coach house; blood dripped from baby Victor's left ear.

Every time Mother told the story, she said she had run out to the street in her blue silk bathrobe and Moroccan slippers, a cigar jammed into the side of her mouth like Mr. Churchill. When I was little, she said the zebras had been so frightened she only had to grab one's mane with her left hand, the other's with her right, and the third zebra followed along like a tired old sheepdog.

But when I was older, she let me know that the zebras reared up and neighed. She lassoed one of them with an old dog leash, another with her belt. The third she wrestled down and tied up with twine, like they did on the ranch in Sonora. She told me one of the zebras kicked her, gave her a gash that needed six stitches.

Mother had a white quarter-moon-shaped scar on her thigh. One day, when we were all swimming at Eden Roc, I asked Victor, "Is that Mother's zebra scar?" When Victor wants to be nasty, he still says, "Is that Mother's zebra scar?" in a high, whiney little voice.

Mother got that scar in 1953. She misjudged a mogul and went flying into a pine tree at Gstaad.

* * *

I call my maid: Bring me a cucumber and a knife.
On each eyelid, I place a slice of cool.

* * *

Mother died last month. Last week I cleaned out her closets. In a cardboard box, underneath a sheaf of letters tied with ribbon, I found a brittle newspaper clipping, so old it had turned orange. It had a picture of Mother in front of the zebra pen at the London zoo. The caption said:

WIFE OF MEXICAN AMBASSADOR BRAVES NAZI BOMBS
FOR LONDON ZOO

She was bundled up in a bulky coat, arms akimbo, her bobbed hair disarranged in a wind. She was squinting, in that funny way she did, her eyes very black, but bright.

* * *

I have an eiderdown quilt. The duvet is Pierre Deux. The ceiling over my bed is a dome made of lightweight bricks which are staggered precisely, row upon curving row, spliced with triangular wedges. When I told the architect I wanted a brick dome for the bedroom, he said it would be difficult: he knew only one man in all the Republic who could make one properly. He was an old Chichimeca who lived in a village in the northern foothills.

Weeks passed.

The Chichimeca arrived in Mexico City without notice, on a thirdclass bus. I did not visit the construction site, but I knew he was there, balancing the bricks in my sky. He would have a wizened brown face and thick white hair. He would know only a few words of Spanish, which he would pronounce strangely, in a high, quavering voice. He would be wearing huaraches, the soles made from a bald car tire, and his toes would be splayed, blackened, twisted.

The dome is beautiful.

Wen Pao, my pug, lies next to me. I stroke her little head. Wen Pao has soft apricot fur. She snores, lightly.

* * *

Three months after the war ended, Mother, Papi, Victor, and the staff were packed off to Buenos Aires. Then Río de Janeiro, then Bogotá, I think, and then Paris, where I was born. I grew up in Grandfather's apartments near the Place des Vosges.

Victor is much older than I. He was thirty when we came back to Mexico in 1968. I was nineteen. I say came back to Mexico, but we had never actually lived there. When I was ten, Grandfather died and we left his apartments on the Place des Vosges and moved to the suburbs, St. Cloud, dreadful. Then the government changed and Papi was posted to Jamaica, Kingston, blistering filth, smells of rotting fruit and butchered animals. Quito, cold and filthy. Tunis: Hellhole on the Mediterranean.

Then Papi died.

Nineteen sixty-eight was a terrible year to be in Mexico, a terrible year to be nineteen. At the time, I thought it was wonderful. Every day was a clean vista, crash of energy and spume.

* * *

Wen Pao leaps to the carpet, barking furiously. My maid shouts through the door, Señora! A boy is selling blackberries from Puebla, 35,000 pesos the kilo. I tell her no—(a reflex)—I saw them for 28,000 at the market yesterday—(pure invention)—but she cannot hear me over Wen Pao's staccato. I stretch. I toss the cucumber slices onto the bedside table.

* * *

Mother promised me the Aubusson carpets. She said that when she died I could have the blue one, the one with the festoons and the gold urns on a robin's-egg blue, a blue (one of the few things I remember Papi saying) like a spring sky over Provence. Mother said I could also have the red Aubusson, which is unevenly faded, and frayed in the center. Knowing Mother, I thought that meant she would leave me the red Aubusson and Victor the blue one. But he got both.

* * *

What did I say? Yes to the blackberries? Would I make a cheesecake with blackberry sauce? Goose stuffed with blackberries? Blackberries served in a crystal bowl with powdered sugar, a pitcher of cream on the side? They would be spooned out into Mother's French porcelain bowls—the white ones with the swirling patterns and the little black stars.

No; I said no.

* * *

We came back to Mexico in 1968. I was nineteen, which is to say I was nothing. Victor had a job with a French investment bank in the Colonia Centro. He also had a wife, a baby, a station wagon, a set of left-handed golf clubs, a cocker spaniel named Tartuffe.

* * *

Papi was on his deathbed in Tunis. He had gone on a three-week trek to see the Roman ruins at Dougga and had suffered an attack of appendicitis in the last week. Mother cried when she read the telegram. That same morning Papi was carried into the Embassy red-faced, screaming. His bed was brought down to the receiving room, which had a marble floor, cooler in the Mediterranean summer. He was sedated. A servant fanned away the flies with an enormous sheaf of palm leaves.

I remember the ceiling there in the receiving room: it was a frieze with rinceaux of acanthus leaves, made of cream-colored plaster. In its corners and center there were putti with tiny wings and monkey-ish faces, all pointing to something out the window: a cinderblock wall. *Belle Epoque à la tunisienne.*

All afternoon Papi lay with his eyes squeezed shut, sweating. Sometimes he groaned, or let out a sharp breath. The boy with the palm fronds wove his arms over the bed like an automaton, hour after hour, his features registering nothing but concentration, rhythm.

I tried to mop Papi's brow with a hand towel I had soaked in lemon water. He flicked open his eyes and waved me away.

Later that same afternoon Mother said, "Well, you are not his child." Just like that.

* * *

There is an earsplitting whistle: the sweet potato man's steamer. He sounds it every day at about this time. Chabelita is home from school, the dishes from lunch have been washed and dried. The traffic has lost the energy of morning, or even early afternoon; now there is only a soft, tired droning. If I were to walk downstairs I might hear the steamer clattering over the cobblestones.

Wen Pao sighs and rolls over onto her side. She splays her paws, like a cat.

Once, when I was small, we came to Mexico City for Holy Week. My nanny bought me a sweet potato. She gave it to me in a dish, with a spoon. We poured honey over it, and heavy cream. Mother came into the kitchen while I was eating it. She said it was a filthy thing, and if I got sick, *ni modo*. Nothing to be done about it.

* * *

We packed our things in Tunis and came to live in Mexico City in 1968. Within a month I'd developed an interest in literature (a crush on Carlos Fuentes), in art history (a yearning to travel in Italy), and in whatever my new boyfriend Esteban might suggest (Asian philosophy, Jimi Hendrix, cannabis, batik wraparound miniskirts).

Mother loved Esteban. She cried more than I did when he was arrested. And it crushed her that when he was released he had changed, become practical.

* * *

So whose child was I? My mother's and only my mother's. I have her curly chestnut hair, her mouth with the puffy upper lip. I have her owlish black eyes. Her thick waist, her ample chest, her tapered fingers, the second toes longer than the big toes. I have her light spray of freckles across the bridge of my nose. And her skin so white my veins show greenish-blue.

And now: I am just beginning to suffer her snowy hairs, that shock of white over my left temple. And too, the crow's-feet, the double chin, the age spots on the backs of my hands.

I have had affairs.

But would I have rescued the zebras from the London zoo?

* * *

The army occupied the university in mid-September 1968. Esteban was picked up in the basement of Philosophy as he was cranking out handbills. He was held incommunicado.

I didn't know what I was doing. I went crazy, shouting at people on the street, the newspaper vendor on the corner, housewives at the supermarket—especially the well-dressed ones, matrons in below-the-knee skirts and big gold Virgin of Guadalupe medals hanging down the middle of their buttoned-up blouses. They'd reach for the Campbell's soup and I'd say, "The students' six demands are perfectly reasonable!"

There was Mother: she wore below-the-knee skirts and had a Virgin of Guadalupe medal hanging down the middle of her buttoned-up blouse. But when I said, "The students' six demands are perfectly reasonable!" she would say, "Yes, of course they are."

The day after Esteban was picked up I took the bus to Victor's office. All the way into the Colonia Centro the bus lurched and rattled. It smelled of greasy food, and of bodies that had been washed, but without soap. I found Victor's office on the fourth floor of a colonial mansion on the Avenida Madero. The secretary showed me a leather couch. I sat there for a long time, crossing and uncrossing my legs.

I curled my lip at the hunting prints, framed in burlwood and black lacquer. I flipped through the annual reports that had been neatly stacked on the coffee table. Their thick glossy paper made me angry. Their photographs of fat men in pinstripe suits made me think of Papi.

I can't remember what I said to Victor. I know I had wanted him to help find out where Esteban was being held. I know I must have cried, said awful things. It was before the massacre at Tlatelolco. He ran an index finger around his little beige hearing aid and took a sip of coffee from his cup, a delicate Limoges.

"Long before you were born," he said, "we had to sleep in the underground, deep down, deeper than any metro in New York, or Paris, or Mexico. The air-raid wardens would sound the sirens and we would gather up water and blankets, playing cards, and a good supply of candles and hurricane lamps. We huddled together for warmth, Mother with me and Papi, the servants and the guards from the Embassy in their olive-green coats. I don't actually remember this," he went on, "nor the drone of the Luftwaffe, the smells in the underground, nor even the whistling sound of the bombs. I just remember how everything was being destroyed. Every day was going to be the end."

He coughed and set his cup on his desk. "One morning Mother was walking me to my school on the other side of St. James. A German pilot had come down without his parachute. There was a tree branch as thick as your waist on the sidewalk next to him. He was nude."

"Victor," I said, "get to the point."

"I kicked his head with my shoe is the point."

I crossed my arms over my chest and looked at him with disgust. "Mother slapped you of course."

"Of course. So I kicked it again."

* * *

Victor was useless. I was unable to rescue Esteban. I remember Mother playing hour after hour of dominoes in the library. She and her friends would nibble chocolates, and she began to spread. The wicker sofa groaned when she got up or sat down. She cried often, and kept a linen handkerchief in her pocket to dab at her eyes.

There was nothing to be done.

They let Esteban out a few days before Christmas. He said the police had lined them up and beat them with their rifle butts. And herded them into a tiny cell without a lavatory.

I was so terribly impressed.

* * *

I married Esteban in 1970; I divorced him in 1972. I have lived as one lives without him since then (marrying twice more, moving to La Jolla once, and back). Mutual friends tell me his management-consulting business is doing well, despite his drinking. His second wife is an American, from Dallas, and she was a nationally ranked golf player. Or a tennis player, I don't recall. Esteban has just made the down payment on a condominium in Cabo San Lucas, overlooking the harbor.

I believe whatever I am in the mood to believe.

* * *

I had a daughter with my second husband, Sebastian. Her name is also Chabela, so I call her Chabelita. Sebastian was killed on the Cuernavaca highway eight and a half months before Chabelita was born. He was changing a tire when a cement truck hit a slick of water and swerved into him.

Mother hated Sebastian. Sebastian owned a chain of American-style steak restaurants. He wore Countess Mara ties, and on weekends, white loafers. He played golf with Victor, and he actually liked the cocker spaniel, Tartuffe. He would stroke Tartuffe's silky muzzle and whisper things in its ears.

"What in God's name are you telling that dog?" Mother thought Sebastian was ridiculous.

When Chabelita was small, Mother would sing her funny songs.

Up above the world you fly,
Like a teatray in the sky.

She would ask her riddles: "Why is a raven like a writing desk?" Once, Mother asked Chabelita the riddle of the Sphinx. Mother searched her little face, and tucked her curls behind her ears. "Why it's woman!" she said, and kissed Chabelita's fat baby cheeks.

* * *

When I was five years old, and Victor sixteen, we were left alone for a weekend in the apartments in Paris. My nanny had left without her pay, I cannot remember why; Papi was in Mexico, Mother had gone to ski in Gstaad. Victor tried to entertain me with his jigsaw puzzle collection, unsuccessfully, because when I couldn't fit the pieces together I would force them. When he took my work apart I cried and punched him. Then he shut me up in my bedroom, but I howled until the neighbors in the opposite building called to complain.

Then Victor got the idea that we should dig up the tiny garden out back, searching for treasure. We dug around and under every single bush and plant, and even poked a spade in between the roots of an old tree. It was a cold and dirty business, but we worked all afternoon Saturday, and the greater part of Sunday. The amazing thing is, Victor actually found something. Behind a pruned rosebush, he unearthed a rotted leather bag of silver coins.

When Mother returned on Monday morning, we found her

hunched over a steaming cup of Turkish coffee, her eyes squeezed shut. Victor emptied the coins out on the breakfast table. They made sharp clicks and thuds on the blackened oak surface, and Mother's eyes opened very bloodshot, very wide. She almost spit out her coffee. "You've stolen them," she said flatly. Victor was indignant. He kicked a leg of the table, too hard. He hopped away biting his lip. I said, "Mother! We dug them up in the garden!" And suddenly she smiled at me so warmly. "The war," she whispered, as if to herself, and began to laugh. I think that was the last moment I loved her without reserve: I climbed on her lap and clasped my arms around her neck. Her face was tanned, her cheeks windburned. She smelled of calamine lotion and hot coffee.

From the corner by the sideboard, Victor said, "They are *my* coins."

"Why?" Mother said, and she scooped them off the table into her purse.

* * *

After Sebastian's funeral I went back to our apartment and sat on the bed. I should have thrown the curtains open; perhaps that simple gesture would have saved me. But I sat on the bed, weighted down as if by stones, and as the afternoon slipped by I could no longer recall his face or his voice. I knew his features by rote—the curve of his chin, the tufts of coarse hair on his earlobes, the oblong mole on his cheek. But they were like scattered pieces of a puzzle; they didn't fit, they didn't make a whole. I remembered that he liked to sing along with his Lucha Villa records; I remembered that as he went out the door to work he always winked and said, "Ciao, baby." But his words ran through my mind in my own voice, as if I were reading aloud from strips of paper. And somehow it chilled me that his clothes were still hanging next to mine in the closet, that his credit cards and cuff links were lying in a box under my shoes.

Mother had to come take care of me. She plumped the pillows and made me lemongrass tea. She brought glossy magazines and she turned the pages for me. She brushed my hair with slow gentle strokes.

Days later, when I was well enough to get up and put on my bathrobe, I saw that Mother had taken all of Sebastian's things from the closet. And when I went to brush my teeth I found that she had removed all the medicines, even the aspirin.

* * *

On Chabelita's tenth birthday Mother gave her a leather pouch. It was new and supple, and quite heavy. Chabelita untied the strings and emptied it over the carpet: out tumbled ten silver coins the size of sand dollars.

I bent down and picked one up. It was a Mexican coin, with a sunburst and a lumpy cap. LIBERTAD, it said. Liberty. On the obverse was the eagle perched on a cactus, a snake writhing in its beak—but with a Chinese character crudely stamped into its wing.

Mother was beaming at Chabelita. "You see those Chinese stamps? There was a time when the peso was worth something."

"Now pesos are for spending," I said. I thought that was terrifically witty.

"You must hide them in a safe place," Mother was telling Chabelita, "but in a place where you won't forget them."

Suddenly I realized: these were the coins Victor and I had dug up in that garden.

Chabelita held one of the coins in her palm, rotating it as she read the minute lettering. "Why would I forget them, Grandma?"

She looked exactly like I did at that age.

* * *

Sebastian was killed eight and a half months before Chabelita was born. I had been seeing his brother. He was a politician with the PAN, always running, always losing. He made his money in plastic tubing. We met on Tuesdays at the Camino Real. We ordered room service.

After the funeral, his brother wouldn't speak to me. Later Mother told me he'd given his house to the Opus Dei.

"*Que pendejo,*" she said. What an ass.

* * *

The week before Mother died, I was in New York with my lover, Karl. My husband, my third husband, my current husband, Juventino, was in London with Victor, on business. I told him I had to shop.

"Shop till you drop," Juventino said.

* * *

I bought this eiderdown quilt there, at a boutique on East 63rd Street. I had a devil of a time getting it into my suitcase. Karl and I jumped up and down on the suitcase to flatten the feathers.

The Pierre Deux duvet, I bought in New York as well.

My robin's-egg blue Aubusson, at auction.

And Wen Pao, my furry baby. She was the smallest in a litter of pugs we saw in a pet shop window on East 78th Street. When she saw us walking by, she stood up on her hind legs, her front paws pressed against the glass.

Karl gave me her red ostrich leather Hermès collar.

We walked Wen Pao in Central Park, every day for a week. It was early November and the leaves were still brilliant orange, burnt sienna, the red of Wen Pao's collar. The air was sharp and clean, and bittersweet with the smell of pretzels and roasting chestnuts. "*Liebling,*" Karl would whisper in my ear, and nudge the nape of my neck, brush his chill lips across my cheek, "*Steh Kopf.*" Stand on your head. Nonsense. *Dance the mambo. Make me a frog leg sandwich with this American ketchup.* But I would return his kiss, his clear-eyed gaze, that satisfied laugh that will always make me think of salted chestnuts shaken in a newspaper cone. We held hands as we shuffled through the brittle leaves, my buttery deerskin glove against his, rough and black. When Wen Pao tired, Karl would pick her up and carry her in his coat.

On the last day we were walking behind the bandshell when I thought I saw Mother with a black man, Rollerblading down East Drive. Her snowy hair, thick waist, and ample chest, her back still strong though curved with years. She was wearing striped stretch pants and a white sweatshirt that said FREE THE— I could not read the rest; she disappeared around a bend.

"*Das bist du,*" Karl said, pointing at her, laughing. Just like you.

* * *

Mother died of a stroke in Mexico City the following week. I found her suitcases piled in the foyer, still packed. I tore off all the luggage tags. Kennedy, Orly, Gatwick, and two others I didn't recognize.

Victor asked me where she was going; I said I had no idea.

* * *

Those letters I found in her closet, tied with silk ribbon: I burned them, one by one. Postmarked Rangoon, postmarked Berlin, London, Lugano. 1927, 1987. Brittle ivory foolscap, red block-letter stamps, browned fountain pen ink, a black wax seal, cracked through the center. Words floated out at me: *Rue, dear, raining very hard since Easter, love, will you? have you? Gstaad, this damn war.* I stared at the flame and let my eyes water. Had I read them?

I might have.

* * *

I see my life in leopard print: spotted with black spots. Tan background, tan like the Sahara desert, like butterscotch pudding, the color of my maid's face.

I bury my face in the fur of Wen Pao's scruff.

Victor looks old now. He has a wattle under his chin. His hair is white, running around the rim of his scalp like a stripe. His bald spot has grown.

"Is that Mother's zebra scar?"

I wish I had never asked him.

* * *

Out my bedroom window the sky is electric orange. If I could see through my brick dome, the sky would be a starless indigo. I have to do my nails, crimson. I have to set my hair. I will wear my gray wool Louis Ferraud, my faux pearls, my Chanel wristwatch, a few daubs of Joy de Patou. Juventino will pick me up for a dinner at the German Embassy, where they will serve us canapés and champagne next to the Christmas tree. There will be a quartet playing Haydn and Handel, and everywhere, the sweet musky perfume of beribboned swags and beeswax candles. Then we will sit in the dining room, for goose with blackberry sauce, Black Forest cake, coffee and liqueurs. Karl is the Ambassador. I think I'll tell his wife about the London zoo.

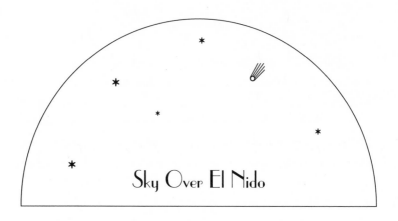

Sky Over El Nido

Rosita conceded that torturers playing trucco *with their prisoners was weird . . .*
Marguerite Feitlowitz "Night and Fog in Argentina"

Figueroa was the fat one. He was the one who always remembered the maple syrup (colored Karo, actually) on Sundays.

We would call to him through the bars, "Figueroa, Figueroa, did you forget the maple syrup?"

For some reason, Figueroa thought this was tremendously funny. When he laughed he would lick his teeth and his belly would jiggle. Sometimes he had to hike up his trousers—with his left hand; he balanced our tray of waffles with the right.

Guzmán was the one with pimples: large pus-filled boils on the back of his neck. His nose looked like a beak. He kept a kerchief in his back pocket.

"Fuck the maple syrup," Guzmán would sneer as he stalked down the corridor. "Fuck it. Fuck you." His heavy black boots would thud by, then echo like the hard flaps of a trapped bird.

* * *

To pass the time, Diego and I told each other stories about Figueroa. My story began like this: Figueroa lives with his mother, in a two-bedroom bungalow that smells of soap and lemons. They listen to public radio together, and he cooks her waffles. Figueroa also washes and irons their sheets, and makes their beds. He sweeps the floors, rinses the dishes, tends the herb garden. After a late supper, he takes her rheumatic Pekinese, Adolph, for a walk around the block.

Diego's story went like this: Figueroa lives alone, in a little room with a low ceiling, a sixth-floor walk-up. Figueroa has to use a bathroom that is down the hall. He has a closet full of women's shoes, all stolen. He subscribes to a foot-fetishist magazine, which arrives more or less every other month, in a brown paper wrapper.

* * *

"What is the name of the magazine?" I asked.

Diego was thoughtful.

We smoked.

The striped shadow cast by the window stretched across the floor. It inched up the gray blanket on Diego's cot. It touched his pillow.

"*Pump,*" he said.

* * *

On Tuesday, Figueroa brought us our dinner: oatmeal with chunks of broccoli stalks. We have been here for many years. We are not sure how many.

"Why not *Spike?*" I said. I picked out the chunks of broccoli and ate them first.

Diego slurped his oatmeal. Diego always leaves the chunks until last. He said, "*Stiletto* perhaps."

* * *

On Wednesday, Figueroa brought us our lunch: boiled rice with sauerkraut. Our cell is lit with a dim 60-watt bulb, but we both spotted the bruise on Figueroa's left cheek. It was the size of an owl's eye.

While we were eating, Guzmán came up and shone his flashlight on our faces. "Bon appetit," he said sweetly. "So sorry you couldn't share the breast of pheasant in mushroom sauce." Then he stomped down the corridor, clanging his flashlight against the bars.

I began: "It was a dark and stormy night."

"Was it?" Diego licked his fingers.

"I thought I heard rain last night, didn't you?"

"No."

* * *

On Thursday, Figueroa brought us our lunch: hot dog buns with golf sauce. His bruise had turned light green, but it was the same size. We ate.

I continued: "After Figueroa had taken Adolph the Pekinese out for his evening walk, they were soaked. Adolph looked like a used kitchen mop. This aggravated his rheumatism. He made a wee-wee on the corner of Figueroa's mother's living room sofa. Figueroa yanked the leash. He said, 'No! Bad doggy!' and smacked Adolph on the haunch. Adolph growled and leapt up. He bit Figueroa on the cheek."

We smoked.

Diego said, "And so, Adolph bit the cheek that fed him. So to speak."

* * *

Figueroa brought us our dinner: deviled kidney on saltines. Figueroa's bruise was still the size of an owl's eye.

Diego said, "Figueroa was sitting on his rumpled bed in his one-room apartment on the sixth floor. It smelled of stale laundry and old newspapers. He read a personal ad on the back page of *Pump*. It said, 'I have nifty little feet, soft as English rose petals, and on my left foot

I have an extra toe.' It gave a telephone number. Figueroa called. A deep voice answered. He immediately thought: Oh my God, this is a transvestite. But then he told himself, Figgy old boy, it's just that she's been smoking unfiltered cigarettes all her life."

Figueroa brought us our dessert, a Twinkie. It was my turn to pull the Twinkie apart. I have rather less talent than Diego; my half had more creme filling.

We heard the buzzing noise, like a bumblebee in front of a microphone. A woman screamed.

It stopped. We smoked.

Diego continued: "So Figueroa made a date: Monday night, at her apartment. He arrived, she let him in. She was wearing big black orthopedic shoes. He knelt down and unlaced them. She *did* have an extra toe on her left foot! Her feet *were* as soft as English rose petals! Figueroa was in ecstasy! He lifted her up and took her over to the bed. He brushed his lips over her ankles, he kissed the soles of her feet. He darted his tongue between her toes. He nibbled and sucked the twisted little extra toe." Diego coughed. "I cannot go on."

"Go on," I said.

Diego lit another cigarette. He exhaled, and we watched the thin smoke filter through the bars of our window. A cluster of stars winked in the twilight.

"Afterwards, the woman went to sleep," Diego said. "Very carefully, very quietly, Figueroa slid open the doors to her closet. She had rows and rows of stiletto-heel pumps, all covered in blue silk. Each heel was as long and sharp as the bill of a heron. 'How can I ever leave?' Figueroa asked himself. 'How?' He climbed into her bed. He rested his feet on her goose-down pillow, next to her face. He felt the whiffs of her little snores on his insteps. He cradled her rose petal feet and began to dream."

* * *

On Friday at dawn Guzmán threw a pail of icy black water through the bars. It landed on the cement floor between our cots.

"You want coffee?" he screamed. "Lap it off the floor!"

We spent the morning watching the coffee evaporate.

By lunchtime there was only a bark-colored splotch.

Diego said, "When Figueroa would not leave, the woman popped him on the cheek with one of her stiletto-heel shoes."

We smoked.

An airplane passed by, the sound of its jet engines arcing across the bowl of the sky. We searched our window, but we could not find the plane.

There was no lunch.

I said, "Birds of a feather don't always stay together."

There was no dinner.

* * *

On Saturday, Figueroa brought us our dinner: soft-boiled eggs. His bruise was a livid yellow. He watched us eat. He had a benevolent expression, which made me think of his mother's herb garden. In a sunny patch of her garden, behind the forest-green iron lawn furniture, she would keep tubs of basil and borage and sage. Insects hum and buzz around a clump of gladiolas; a robin has its nest up in the crook of the roof. Watercress sprouts from coffee cans scattered under a leafy walnut tree. (Adolph would be tethered in the garage.) And in the kitchen, on a ledge over the sink, tiny clay pots of rosemary, chive, and lemon balm rest on saucers.

Diego winked at me and wiggled his toes.

Figueroa held out his hand through the bars. It was hammy, hairy.

We passed him our eggshells. He smiled and licked his teeth as he balled his fist, crushing the shells. Then he walked down the corridor.

We smoked.

Figueroa was back. He hiked his trousers. "Inge!" he called. A little girl, perhaps ten years old, came shuffling up. She had a pixie cut, and her eyes were set close together. She curled her hands around the bars, delicate as the claws of a wren. She stared at us.

Figueroa said, "These are the ones I've been telling you about, Princess." He pointed. "This is Diego, and the other one . . ."

"Hernán," I said.

"Diego and Hernán," Figueroa said. "They like waffles with maple syrup." He laughed that big belly laugh, his thumbs in the belt loops of his trousers.

The little girl blinked. She said, "Pleased to meet you."

Figueroa patted her on the head. Then he took her by the hand and led her away.

* * *

On Sunday morning we heard loud clattering footsteps. It was Guzmán and Figueroa, together. Figueroa carried the tray of waffles and a small white pitcher with our maple syrup.

Because Guzmán was with him, we did not call to Figueroa through the bars about the maple syrup.

Guzmán squeezed the back of his neck. Then he whipped out the kerchief and dabbed at it. "You can go now," he said quietly. "The Governor says you are both free to go."

This had happened before. "Figueroa," I said, "did you forget the maple syrup?"

Figueroa passed the tray to Guzmán. He held up his trousers with both hands and began to laugh. Guzmán hurled the tray against the wall. Shards of crockery flew through the clammy air like a spray of stars.

Figueroa laughed and laughed, until his face turned red and tears welled in his eyes. The syrup ran down the wall, sweet rain oozing through the plaster.

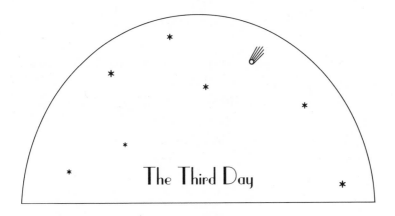

The Third Day

The night Jane lost the skin on her fingertips, she saw a boy hanging upside down from a tree. The light was pink with summer, the breeze carried the scent of gasoline and freshly mowed grass. The boy's T-shirt had slipped down to expose a swath of molasses-colored skin and a large and knotty belly button. He was making big circles with his arms. Somewhere a stereo blared out "Stairway to Heaven"; guitar riffs and a soft drumbeat wove into the breeze.

In the morning Jane wakes to find herself buried in the snow. Her foxhole is still loose powder, fallen in close on her sleeping bag, but the warmth of her breath has left a smooth hollow. Jane can see this hollow because she is buried by only a thin film and the day is piercing yellow, ocean blue, and white.

Something vinyl black hits her in the face. It's Bobby, frantically digging her out.

"Jane!" he shouts. "Jane!"

She cries out like a small animal. Everything is slow.

"I'm sorry," Bobby says, startled. His voice seems to evaporate in the thin air. Jane twists herself into a sitting position. Bobby is standing in powder up to his knees and his face is somehow sore and gray at the same time. His lips are slathered white. His black mittens flop impatiently on his thighs like boxer's gloves.

He already has his backpack on.

Jane's eyes are slits in the snowblink. She pulls her hands out of the sleeping bag, stiff and raw in their mittens.

"You're sorry," she whispers.

"What?"

"You're sorry." Her voice is brittle. A strand of hair rakes her cheek, frozen straw.

* * *

They had started out on a partly cloudy morning, a day Bobby said might turn, a day she knew would turn. "Bobby, it's gonna turn," she had said, tugging at his sleeve when they were still in the parking lot.

"I've climbed Mt. Shasta," he reminded her, fiercely. "I've looked into the steaming crater of Popocatepetl." He had traveled the back roads of Guerrero on his motorcycle. Now they were going to cross-country ski to a hut fifteen miles away. They had brought a map. They had brought sleeping bags and matches. They had brought sunblock and fruitbars.

They had begun to ski.

* * *

Jane does not get up. The day is enormous, soundless; cirrus clouds are brushed into the deepest wells of sky.

"Oh Bobby," Jane says, staring at her soggy mittens, "I don't think I'm gonna make it."

"Don't be a quitter," he says, his mouth a ragged ring of white.

Jane tries to remember that Bobby has twine-colored curly hair. She tries to imagine him laughing, his tongue darting along the salted rim of a margarita. She tries to imagine him riding his motorcycle. Then she remembers her vision of the brown-skinned boy. His hair had hung down straight. His arm had swung down, and with one finger he had drawn a circle in the dust.

"Haaa, haaa." Bobby is breathing into his metal camp cup, trying to melt some snow to drink. In a moment the cup holds a few swallows of liquid and only a teaspoon-sized lump of snow. Bobby passes her the cup and she drinks. An icy river slides down her throat and coats the lining of her stomach. Bobby has his goggles on now, and when she looks at him she sees her reflection, warped and small.

This is the third day, the day he will find the unlocked forest station. The day he will stamp H-E-L-P in the snow outside the latrine, hang the flag upside down from the roof. The day he will break up the furniture he finds inside and warm his hands over a fire.

* * *

The first day, they had begun to ski through a narrow valley ringed with jagged boulders and pine-dotted slopes. A thread of river ran through it, gurgling over the stones like a silly conversation. The air smelled of pine needles and sweet water, and scattered snowflakes floated down like cotton puffs. Jane caught one on her tongue. They skied side by side, their skis and poles and breathing making a quiet *tick-sloosh, tick-sloosh* over snow that was smooth and firm. Soon Bobby lost patience with her pace. Then she followed in his tracks, watching his legs scissor back and forth, his pole baskets throw out tufts of white. They skied through another valley, along the bank of the river through a meadow, and another field where Bobby skied farther and farther ahead of her, until she shouted from nearly half a mile back, "Hey, Bobby! Wait up!"

They stopped after two hours to eat fruitbars. Jane perched on an outcropping of granite; Bobby stabbed his poles into the snow and stretched his arms wide. "Can you dig this?" He grinned and let out a yell that ricocheted through the valley like a yodel. "If I had my guitar!" And he grabbed one of his poles out of the snow and played air-guitar on it. " 'Stairway to Heaven'!" He laughed. "Wick-ed!"

They were near the fork in the river, where they planned to ski up a wide pass through steep and craggy slopes, then an easy trek down towards the hut by the lake. Here all the trees were stripped on one side and the branches pointed downhill. It had begun to snow now, big sloppy blobs that slid off their waterproof parkas but landed wet on Jane's red wool mittens.

"That was stupid," Bobby said, glancing at her mittens, scanning the broken trees. "Now your hands will freeze."

Suddenly the temperature dropped. The gold plastic wrapper of her fruitbar flew out of her hand into the snow. She reached down to pick it up, but another gust blew it tumbling over a drift and into the river. The air had turned a dense silvery gray. Bobby grunted and tucked his crumpled wrapper into his backpack.

As they skied towards the pass the snow began to fall faster and drier. The wind began to whip up whirls of snow, and they could no longer see the trees at the tops of the slopes, or the thread of river. Soon they were pushing through drifts that were ankle deep, knee deep, and in places, waist deep. Jane felt as if she were being shaken in a bubbledome filled with water and plastic flecks. She clenched her poles tight. She was not worried though, yet. Bobby had told her he spent the night in a snow cave once, when he was on Mt. Shasta. "Sounds bad," he had said, knocking back a margarita. "But it's no big deal." Bobby had a map. They had sleeping bags and matches.

Then they could not even see the tips of their skis. The wind lashed around her goggles, seared her forehead, cut to the bone beneath her cheeks. They called to each other through the howling and whistling, "Where are you?" Her fingers were stinging as if she had plunged them into boiling water. "Where are you?" Suddenly she saw the yellow of his parka. She grabbed his arm, fell on top of him.

"Shit!" Bobby was swearing. "Holy shit!" Without trying to stand up, he started throwing out handfuls of snow. "Dig!" he screamed in the crazy whirl. "We've got to make a snow cave!" But the snow was like dry sand.

He was panicking. Jane wanted to panic, but she pulled him down again. "Take off your skis," she commanded. "Lie here, close to me." He threw his arms around her shoulders and held her like a vise. His breathing was deep and fast; she felt it on her throat, in and out, hot, chill. His chest heaved against hers, her lips brushed the coarse stubble on his chin. Quickly, quickly, the snow covered them like a blanket. She whispered, "Let's get into our sleeping bags," and blindly they wrestled themselves into their bags, curled up with their knees to their chins. She clenched her eyes shut against the white, wet wool, heart pounds and wind and white.

* * *

It must have been hours later. The snow was still falling, but the wind had died and they could make out the forms of trees lining what they thought was the pass. The sky was low and the light was dimming. The pine trees, the outcroppings of rock, the river, were all shrouded in one thick sheet. Bobby pulled out his map, but it was hard to read in the snowfall and failing light. He held it one way, and then another. He squinted out into the mists.

"If only we could see the river," Jane said in a strangely high voice. Out of her sleeping bag, she had begun to shiver violently.

"That way," Bobby said, and gave the map a *thwat* with his mitten.

In every direction, Jane saw the same shrouded slopes. "Maybe we should orient ourselves to the sun," she said, holding herself tightly.

Bobby snickered, "What sun?"

She had meant to say, "The light," but there was only an even, diffused clamshell gray.

"Follow me," he said.

* * *

Now, on the third day, Jane sits dazzled in the early light, tears slicing her cheeks like razors. Bobby is telling her that he can't wait much longer, that they have to use the light. She is trying to remind herself that Bobby sells something—computers, or restaurant supplies, or was it new bank accounts? She is trying to remind herself that she has a job in a travel agency. That she has a Formica-top desk with a telephone, a fax, a vase of brilliant paper flowers. That the Friday before she left with Bobby she had sold a honeymoon couple a cruise down the Mexican Riviera. They would leave from Los Angeles and stop first at Cabo San Lucas. Jane has seen dozens of brochures with photographs of the arches at Cabo. The ocean always sparkles blue, and the sky looks like the ocean, brushed with coconut milk. There are always seals and pelicans, and a little boat, passing through the putty-colored arch.

"I'm not gonna carry you, Jane." Bobby jabs his poles in the snow. He lifts his chin and looks down the valley, two flashing stars of sun on his goggles.

"I'm not gonna pull you down from there," Jane whispers to the boy, who is still hanging upside down.

Bobby does not hear her. He is chewing the last fruitbar.

"You can stay there like that all day," she whispers. "I don't care." There is a faint rustling; through her face, her palms, ankles, a livid shimmer of heat. "But doesn't your head hurt?" The boy shakes his head. "Isn't the blood pounding in your eyes?" The boy blinks; he tugs his T-shirt back up and tucks it into his shorts. "Why don't we go do something else?"

"Like what?" And the boy has already landed on his bare feet in the dust. He is a Mexican boy, his head as high as her chest.

"We could play angels on the roof."

There is a sudden rip of machine noise.

"I gotta help my dad mow the lawn."

"No you don't."

"NO! NO! NO!" Bobby is screaming. He is kicking out snow as he tries to jump in the drifts. "NO! DAMN!" A helicopter, small as a fat black fly, disappears over the skyline.

* * *

On the second day, Jane and Bobby woke to the sound of a low far-away rumbling. The morning was still a starless black. The rumbling became a bass drumroll, snare, then a cracking earsplitting thunder. Briefly: a sound like the trickle of a fountain. Jane jerked out of her sleeping bag, gasping, blind. Bobby's voice was small and tight. "It's not nearby," he said. "Go back to sleep. Save your energy." He was somewhere to her left. He coughed. "Happens all the time when there's a lot of snow."

All day the second day it snowed heavily, dry small flakes swirling in the wind. Her feet felt like frozen lumps, the backs of her hands flayed to tendon and bone, and when the gusts lashed her ribs, her spine, she felt as if she were skiing in the nude. Bobby had decided they would ski towards the highway, about five miles east of the river. By late morning they were pushing through a vast field of waist-high drifts, their skis and poles on their shoulders. Pain shot through her thighs, and the heavy skis and poles cut into the thin flesh on her shoulders and collarbone. She tried to pretend that the snow was flour; then, that the blizzard was a sirocco of hot sand. She tried to imagine sudsy warm milk baths, thick cotton towels, fist-sized soaps in the shape of clamshells. She tried to remember the words to songs that she had heard on the radio, that Bobby whistled under his breath when he was bored.

Soon the wind was blowing her over, sideways, backwards.

"Leave your skis," Bobby shouted back through the flurries. "They're weighing you down. Let's go!"

She dropped the skis and the poles one on top of the other. They made a black *X* and sank in the powder.

"Bobby," Jane cried, "it's been more than five miles!"

He was already pushing ahead. She watched his back fade into the gauze of flurries. She sneezed and lurched forward, her legs heavy as sacks of sand, her hips chafing against the snow. Along the surface of the snow fields, the wind made curlicues and tendrils, rippling whorls. And then she felt her pack with the sleeping bag, the fruitbars, the sunblock rubbing her shoulder blades, the small of her spine, heavy as a bag of stones. She fell to her knees.

"Bobby, it's been more than five miles!" The sound of her voice was crushed in the heavy air. She watched his poles bob on his shoulders, farther and farther ahead. A whiffet tipped her forward and she let go, let her cheek nestle into the powder. She felt nothing; her face was completely numb. Suddenly she realized that she was very thirsty. She pressed down her chin and took in a mouthful of snow. A stabbing pain in her teeth, the roof of her mouth: for a driblet.

Bobby was standing over her.

"Bobby!" she said with her eyes clenched shut. "We're lost."

He scraped his skis off his shoulder and hurled them into the snow. Jane listened for his breathing; she only heard whistling through jagged boulders and snow-laden pines. Her eyes, her calves, her forearms burned. Then Bobby said something, very softly. Her heart was racing; she could not hear what it was.

* * *

Now, on the morning of the third day, Jane sits dazzled in the snow, trying to remember how it was that she met Bobby. She sinks down on an elbow and curls up small, her knees cupped in the soft underside of her chin. She tries to remember what color shirt Bobby was wearing, what Bobby was drinking, which song was playing on the jukebox. She tries to remember what it was that he must have said to her. Matted strands of hair play across her eyes.

"You're so much fun, Jane." She sees the boy again. He is standing in the dust, rubbing the sole of one foot along his other knee. He is pulling his faded blue T-shirt with his thumbs, smiling shyly.

"Let's go in your house," she says.

"Okay." The boy's hand is warm in hers. He leads her in through the kitchen, where something that smells of corn and boiling salted water simmers on the stove. They walk through a hallway that has cabbage rose wallpaper, stained and peeling; up a narrow flight of stairs. Their shoulders brush the grimy walls; the planks creak and groan.

"To get to the roof we have to use the big bedroom," the boy says. They are on the landing now, breathing heavily.

"Is it this one?" she asks, jiggling a doorknob.

"No." The door clicks open. Inside, there is an unmade bed and the odor of dirty sweatclothes and sneakers; tattered gray curtains billow out the window. "No," the boy says again. "This is my brother's room."

She walks in and sits on the bed. She looks blankly at the boy, who stays in the hallway. The sheets are thin and faded, as if they have been washed again and again. A shiny black electric guitar lies on the floor, a rainbow-hued strap tangled around its neck; on the wall, a poster of a blonde woman in a red bikini, riding a motorcycle.

"That's my brother's guitar," the boy says. "He can play as good as the records."

"Good," Jane says. "That's good." She stands up. "Let's go to the big bedroom."

The boy leads her to the other side of the landing, where a rectangle of rose-yellow light seeps out onto the carpet like a puddle. "This is the room," he says.

She pushes open the door. A lumpy king-size bed with a faded lavender spread takes up most of the floorspace. Above the headboard, pinned up with thumbtacks, is a portrait of Jesus. An enormous white tear runs down his olive-brown cheek. An unvarnished vanity is wedged into a corner. It is covered with vials of perfume samples, drugstore lotions, travel-sized plastic bottles of shampoo, lipsticks, brilliant pink, crimson, purple. A vase of fresh-cut daisies. Jane squeezes herself in between the bed and the vanity. Suddenly she sweeps her arm across the top of the vanity. The bottles and the vase fall in a clatter to the floor.

"I had to find the radio," she says, without looking at the boy. The radio is a small flat box. She switches it on and the tinny bleat of tropical music fills the room. She hops up onto the bed; she jumps, she twists. The little room is hot as an oven. The boy stays in the doorway, biting his lip. Jane notices that his blue T-shirt has some writing on it, so faded she cannot read it.

"Hey!" she says, her hair flying. "What does your T-shirt say?"

The boy looks down at his chest as if for the first time. He holds his shirt out with his thumbs. "'I heart Baby Shamu,'" he says. "It's from Sea World."

"Well!" Her heart is pounding like a jackhammer. "I heart Baby Shamu too!" And she pulls him by the wrists up onto the bed, swings his arms to the beat of the marimba, *donk, dink, donk.* They jump, they shimmy to the frenzy of the maracas.

"Caaa-lifornia Fruitbars, six bars of sun to a box!" A commercial has come on. They flop down on the sheets, the lavender spread now kicked into a wrinkled heap on the floor. Jane breathes the words: "To play angels on the roof, you have to take the sheets off the bed."

"Can we do that?"

"It's okay, don't worry." She rips the top sheet off. "Stand up," she says, and gives the boy a shove. She throws the sheet over him and for a brief moment it puffs out like a parachute, then falls and clings to his shoulders. The boy spreads his arms and smiles. His teeth are tiny and pointed, as if they have been filed.

Jane pulls back the curtains and unlatches the window. Beyond the line of the roof, a giant oak stands to one side, surrounded by a ring of dust; its lush gray-green leaves glisten in the breeze. And then there is grass: fields and fields of grass, swaying, rippling. To the horizon, grass.

"I told you," the boy says. "I gotta cut the grass."

"Yes." The sky looks yellow. Jane scans the sky, but there is no sun. She grabs the boy's waist, lifts him over the windowsill and onto the roof. He lands unsteadily and starts to whimper. He cradles his foot.

"I got a splinter!"

"Jump," Jane says.

His chin is a quivering knot of flesh. He stares at her, cocks his head slightly, as if trying to remember something. Then he begins to step gingerly, slowly, towards the edge. Halfway down, his sheet catches between the shingles; he yanks it out and keeps stepping, stepping. At the edge, his small brown toes curl around the shingles. He looks back at Jane.

"Go ahead."

"Okay, then." This is Bobby's voice. Bobby's face. Goggles. Black, shiny. Piercing yellow, ocean blue, white like bedsheets. His breath is rank.

"It's okay," Jane says. She has nothing left in her voice.

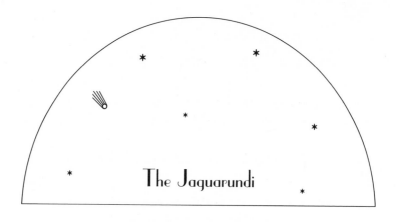

The Jaguarundi

mirror, mirror, on the page
have you known a happier age?
and deliver us from rage
and keep tigers in their cage
Carlos Fuentes

I was sitting on Manette's faded chintz sofa when the jaguarundi rubbed its flank against my calf. I paid it no notice, thinking it was a house cat. Later, when I was leaving, I saw it curled up atop one of Uwe's music boxes. Its head was as long and flat as a weasel's, and its coat was a dusty black, like an otter's.

"That's my jaguarundi," Manette said as she passed me my umbrella. It flicked open its eyes at the sound of her voice. They were larger than a cat's, coffee-colored, with round pupils.

"Uwe bought her for me from a rancher in Chiapas," Manette was saying. "I'm painting her into my 'jungle pastiche.' Uwe's written a poem about her, '*Gibt es einen Zoo in der Nähe?*' "

"You know I can't understand a word of German," I said and I kissed her on the mouth.

This was in Coyoacán, an old neighborhood of Mexico City. This was 1982, when we all had dollars in the Mexican banks and we all felt rich, or rich enough anyway. Uwe was importing music boxes from Austria and Denmark, brought in on some politician's private plane to avoid paying duty. Manette had begun to sell her jungle paintings through a gallery in the Zona Rosa. I had most of my money parked with my father's stockbroker in New York; in Mexico I lived simply, in work shirts and blue jeans, no furniture, a portable typewriter. If I needed a tie, I didn't go.

I began to go to Manette's house nearly every afternoon. We drank shot glasses of prickly pear brandy, or tequila with a spritz of lime; once, we drank a finger of Uwe's peppermint schnapps and smoked a joint. Manette's jaguarundi lolled on the apricot kilim at our feet, it's purr deep and rough. The rains started by about four, and they made the jaguarundi restless. It would leap from music box to music box, to the ledge over the sofa where it set Uwe's Zapotecan bowls wobbling and spinning. Sometimes I caught a glimpse of its tail, much longer, more slender than a cat's, among the forest of antique silver frames on the baby grand piano. When it came near the sofa again, Manette would rake her hand along its back, then lightly, with one finger, along its tail.

"Precious," she always said.

The garden was chill and lush. Manette had hung wind chimes made of abalone shells from the eaves, and it is this that I remember, more than her voice, although that too was soft and flute-like. And I remember the faint smell of ferns and of wet geraniums, the cool lightness of her eiderdown duvet thrown over my back; teak, waxed rosewood, and the jaguarundi that smelled like Manette, tart and sugary, like bramble, or hazelnuts.

Uwe was German. There were a lot of Germans in Mexico, people whose great-grandfathers had confused Galveston with Veracruz, most of them engineers or chicken farmers or accountants. Uwe wrote poetry and sold music boxes. I met him a few weeks after I'd begun to see Manette, at one of his and Manette's Thursday night "open houses."

"So you are a writer," he said. He wasn't really looking at me; he was watching Manette. She had the jaguarundi in her arms and was going around the room, allowing people to pet it. Somehow, Uwe got it out of me that I had lived in Nairobi, and Fez, and a village of exactly seven souls and a flock of bandy-legged sheep on the northwest coast of Skye, and that I had published two chapbooks of poetry, and recently, a collection of travel essays I'd written for a Canadian magazine.

"You are busy, busy, busy," Uwe said. He had jet-black hair, dyed I suspected, and a broken nose. "For you," he said, taking a swallow of his cognac, " 'The Flight of the Bumble Bee.' " He led me to a dark corner in the foyer. Next to the hat stand was a stone pedestal, and on it, an oval-shaped box made of mahogany and polished burlwood; there was a bee the size of my hand on each of its sides, inlaid with obsidian and yellow jade. Uwe wound it up with an iron key.

"I travel light," I laughed. "I don't have a car, I don't even own a tie."

"Does not matter," he said. He knew who my father was. "If you can have a beautiful thing, why not have it?"

The music sounded like the abalone shell chimes in a storm.

"Rimsky-Korsakoff," he said, stroking his chin and smiling tightly, as if in ecstasy. "I will give you a good price."

"No thanks," I said. "But thanks."

* * *

"Uwe's a lousy poet," Manette told me once. We had stepped out of the shower and toweled each other off. She was pulling a tortoiseshell comb through her waist-length blonde hair. "Do you know, he's never published anything?" she said fiercely. "Uwe only knows how to collect things. Things and people."

I had seen the music boxes, the ones Uwe kept for himself; the antique beer steins lined up on a shelf near the living room ceiling, the Zapotecan bowls, the filigreed silver frames, black and white photographs, a basket full of fingernail-sized gold coins stamped with the profile of the Archduke Maximilian.

"God," she said, her eyes glistening. "Even here, in the bathroom." She tapped her comb against the glass on a print. "Uxmal," she said with disgust. She pointed to the print next to the sink. "That one's Chichén." They covered the walls, Sayil, Labná, Dzibilchaltún, Mayan ruins under a hand-colored dawn.

She'd slicked her hair into a rope and was leaning forward, twisting the towel around her head. When she stood up, it was as if she had on a fantastic headdress. Water drops sparkled in the wells of her collarbone.

"Tortoiseshell combs!" she said, grabbing a fistful from a Talavera bowl. "Tin soldiers, politicians, Agustín Lara recordings, poets—"

I ran my hands down her shoulder blades and buried my face in her neck.

I thought I would see another jaguarundi. But I never have, not once in my life.

* * *

Manette never finished what she called her "jungle pastiche" painting. Near the end of the rainy season the president gave a speech everyone who had a television watched. I didn't have a television, but Manette called me that night to tell me that the president had begun to shout, towards the end, about plunder, conspiracies; tears welled in his eyes, he shook his fist at the cameras. He said he would nationalize the banks, and no one was allowed to change pesos for dollars, or dollars for pesos. Uwe hurled one of his beer steins at the screen. The beer stein had been worth a lot of money, Manette said, enough to buy a small car.

Uwe had decided they would go to Vienna, for several months.
"Uwe's taking me to the operas," she mumbled, and began to cry.
"Don't forget your opera glasses," I said.
"Look in on my jaguarundi," she said.
I hung up on her.

I couldn't work for days. I sat on the mattress in my bare apartment, balancing the typewriter on my knees. I drank weak *té de tila*, I smoked stale Marlboros and chewed my nails. I tried to finish a travel piece about the Pacific Coast, but instead I wrote a series of poems I titled "Manette in the Morning," because, I realized, I had never seen her in the morning. Later, when I left Mexico, I would tear them to shreds and flush them down the toilet.

I toured every single church and museum in the city limits, I walked through the Alameda, and Chapultepec Park, looking each woman I saw full in the face. I went to the Chapultepec zoo and threw a hot dog to the tiger. I took the metro to Coyoacán, thinking I might look in on the jaguarundi, but my feet wouldn't take me to Manette's cobblestone lane. I kept walking down Francisco Sosa, past Las Lupitas, through the plaza to El Parnaso where I bought a chapbook by a Mexican poet I'd met on one of those Thursday nights, a short mousy-haired woman I didn't really respect. I stared at her words as I drank a coffee I didn't really want. I left the book face down next to the tip.

Then I did look in on the jaguarundi. The maid let me in, saying she'd been expecting me. She asked me if I wanted a brandy, or a shot glass of tequila. I asked where the jaguarundi was, and she clapped her hands and called its name. But it didn't come.

"It is sad," she said, "now that Señora Manette is gone." Her red and white checked apron was soiled. "It broke one of Señor Uwe's Zapotecan bowls. I had to punish it." She stared at the floor and twisted her braid.

We began to search for the jaguarundi, behind the chintz sofa, around the music boxes, behind the plumería in clay pots painted with the faces of the sun and moon. And in the laundry patio, the garden, the dining room. I went upstairs, to Manette's and Uwe's bedroom. The drapes were closed and Manette's jewelry box was gone, but everything else was the same. There were dusky black hairs shed all over the eiderdown duvet, and a small oval indentation where the jaguarundi had slept on her pillow. I could hear the maid downstairs, still clapping her hands and calling for it. I opened the drapes and pushed out the window. The abalone shells tinkled in the breeze.

Manette's closet door was ajar. I walked in, and I thought I might sink to my knees, drown in the smell of laundered cotton, grassy linen, the oranges she'd stuck with cloves. I grabbed an armful of her blouses and held them to my cheek. The jaguarundi began to purr and to weave between my legs.

It let me pick it up and carry it downstairs to the sofa. I sat with it on my lap for a while, nuzzling it, burying my face in its scruff. Everything was the same, as if Manette and Uwe might be coming home for cocktails any minute. I poured myself a schnapps and wound up the nearest music box, a large dust-covered chest. It played too slowly, missing the A and the F sharp, "Dance des Mirlitons," from *The Nutcracker Suite.* I sat on the sofa for a long time, smoothing the jaguarundi's fur with the flat of my hand, listening for the faint rush of the city's arteries, to the jaguarundi's shallow breath and my own. When I got up to leave, the jaguarundi cocked its head, staring at me.

Outside, the sun was a harsh white, everything was dry.

∗ ∗ ∗

The maid had been giving the jaguarundi cat food and it looked a little thin, so I returned the next afternoon with a fish wrapped in butcher paper. The jaguarundi came dashing up to me when I called it from the foyer, and it put its front paws on my knees, sniffing for the fish. I could feel its claws through my blue jeans, and its eyes shone, even in the dim.

I stood in the kitchen, watching the maid fry the fish in a teaspoon of corn oil, then pick the bones out, then spoon it into the jaguarundi's dish on the tile floor.

"This fish is very expensive," the maid said, wiping her hands on her apron.

"Yes," I said.

I went home and wrote a poem about brambles and hazelnuts, bumblebees, the gossamer blue cast to the winter morning. I started to write Manette a letter, something about the economic recovery program the new president called the PIRE. "Your maid would call it the 'pyre,'" I wrote. Ha ha. I crumpled that one up and tossed it in the trash. I started another letter, about how Francisco Sosa, the main street in Coyoacán, had been cleaned up now that the president's family had their house there, near the bridge over the river and the terra-cotta-colored eighteenth-century chapel. Armed soldiers patrolled the street outside, looking bored, smoking cigarettes. Inflation was more than 200 percent, I wrote her in another letter. There was no sugar or flour in the supermarket. There were campesinos, I told her on the back of a postcard (a garish view of Acapulco by night), who came to the city and drank gasoline and then lit a match and breathed fire. The people in their cars at stoplights gave them coins. I saw this from the window of a public bus. I thought I might go to Chang Mai after Christmas, I wrote, or Marrakesh, or Cairo.

I kept the letters I wrote to Manette in my jacket pocket; the poems I wrote about her, by my bedside table. All through that winter I came to see the jaguarundi in the afternoons; yet somehow, I always forgot to ask the maid for their address.

Manette had left her paints, her brushes, canvases, everything. I couldn't imagine what she was doing in Vienna. Manette didn't read much, or watch television. The opera didn't go on all day. I'd been to Vienna, but still I imagined it as a closed, black damp place where old people huddled in unheated apartments, playing violoncellos.

Her studio was in a padlocked shed at the back of the garden, overgrown with ragged bougainvillea. Through a tiny window I could see the corner of her "jungle pastiche" painting where she had left it on the easel. Pinned on the walls were pencil sketches of the jaguarundi: its head, from different angles, with its eyes shut, opened, its ears sleek against its skull; one hind leg, its rosebud nose, lolling on its back, pouncing on a shard of pottery. With the dry season, though, the bougainvillea blossomed and spread, purple, brilliant orange, and the small room darkened.

I drank all the schnapps and most of the tequila. I smoked the marijuana I found stashed in the bathroom, and I wound up and listened to every single music box. I shuffled through Uwe's black and white photographs: of Indian women in headdresses made of live iguanas; the volcanoes ringed with clouds, like scarves; a snapshot of B. Traven in his library on the Calle Mississippi.

I brought the jaguarundi tuna and huachinango, and once a bit of catnip a friend drove down from Laredo. Soon I didn't have to clap or to call for the jaguarundi; it was waiting for me in the shadows of the foyer at the same hour every afternoon. After it ate, the jaguarundi would pad into the living room and jump up to lie next to me on the sofa. It would lick its whiskers or the pads of its paws; it would purr loudly and flick its tail with contentment. Sometimes the jaguarundi rubbed its chin against my leg, asking me to tickle its ears.

The days passed like this, one after the other, and another. I wrote an article about mariachis for the Canadian magazine, and a sort of philosophical essay on the floating gardens at Xochimilco. I reviewed the galleys for another chapbook. I read travel guides, to India, North

Africa; I considered living in a settlement on the edge of Hudson Bay. And then the rainy season began again, suddenly, with a violent downpour.

"I am sitting in your living room," I scribbled to Manette. I crumpled the paper in my fist.

"I was fucking your wife," I wrote to Uwe.

I asked the maid for their address.

The next afternoon I brought the jaguarundi a stingray. The maid wrinkled her nose at it, but I told her not to worry, the meat was like tuna, only with a slightly sharper, salty taste. Go ahead and boil it, I said, and I went into the living room. I opened the liquor cabinet and lined up what was left: a finger of tequila, anise liqueur, Campari, gin, a shot of the prickly pear brandy. I poured them all into a tumbler. The liquor filled a little more than half the glass. The mixture was a reddish brown, like coagulated blood. I drank it all. Then I sat on the sofa.

When the jaguarundi jumped up, I skidded my hand along its back. I began to kiss it on the scruff, between its eyes, and I hugged it until it cried, until it clawed at me, spat at me and hissed. It wriggled away finally and I staggered into the bathroom and threw up.

"You are singing Oaxaca?" the maid shouted through the bathroom door. Maids would speak this way to foreigners. "You ate some stingray?"

"No!" I shouted, my knuckles white on the edge of the toilet bowl. "I'll be all right," I said. I lost my balance and fell to the floor.

The light was a pale rosy gray when I woke up, with a sour taste in my mouth and a blinding headache. I touched my fingertips to my face: it was crusted with fresh scabs. There was a musty smell, from the eiderdown duvet, I realized, on Manette's bed. I heard the jaguarundi's raspy purr: it was curled at the foot of the bed, watching me carefully. When I sat up, it scampered into the closet, its long tail swishing behind it.

I remembered then that I hadn't yet affixed the postage to those letters. I clapped my hands, once, weakly. I sank back into the pillow and slept until late afternoon. When I left the clouds were a fretwork, spent and drifting. The cobblestones were slick and the air smelled of earth and gasoline.

* * *

Some days later I came back with a pair of plastic earrings for the maid, and a huachinango.

"Ah," the maid said, her eyes very round, as she took the packages. She had on a clean apron. I asked for the jaguarundi. She called out its name, but the jaguarundi did not come. She shrugged. "Would you like a tequila?" she asked.

"But aren't we out of liquor?" I tried to approximate a sheepish look. I had my hands in my pockets.

"Oh," she murmured. She knit her brow, as if she suddenly recognized something large and obvious. She crossed her arms over her chest. "The Señor Uwe is home," she blurted. She seemed to intuit what she needed to say from my expression. "He went to the store," she said, "to buy lightbulbs."

"Thank you," I said, and I left.

The next day I came home to find an enormous canvas wrapped in brown paper standing up against my bed. It was Manette's unfinished "jungle pastiche." Henri Rousseau's lion peeped out from the long grasses; there were myna birds and banana trees, vermilion hawaiianas, and a spider monkey swinging from a vine. Picasso's harlequin sprawled in the ferns, smoking a joint. Manette had painted me and the Venus de Milo waltzing through a blank sky.

I looked for the jaguarundi; she said she'd painted it in, but I couldn't find it.

The next afternoon I flew to Cairo with my duffel bag and my typewriter. I left the landlady my styrofoam coffee cups, a half empty box of laundry detergent, and the painting. I was going to write a series of articles about the River Nile, but I ended up doing something on belly dancers, and the oud, and Anwar Sadat's novel. I ended up spending a winter in Alexandria, writing sonnets; then a couple of years in Tangiers in an apartment behind the souk, with a view of the straits, the swallows, the biscuit-white shores of Spain.

I didn't think much about Mexico. It seemed exotic, the farther away I was from it, like Cairo itself, the wildly colored turbans the women wore in Nairobi, like an emerald twilight. Every once in a while the *International Herald Tribune* would print a few column inches about Mexico with a photograph of a high-rise beach hotel or a woman picking through a mountain of garbage. I read that there were earthquakes in Mexico City in 1985. I was worried, and I considered calling, but then I met someone on a plane who told me most of the damage was in the Colonia Centro, where cheap hotels and rotting palaces and *vecindades* were built over the ancient lake bed. The earthquakes hadn't affected Coyoacán, which was on volcanic rock. The price of crude oil fell, drastically, the president was booed and heckled at the World Cup Soccer matches. The fans trashed the Sanborn's where I used to go to buy American magazines. A team of fresh-faced economists with names like Téllez Kuenzler and Carstens was renegotiating the foreign debt.

I suppose I could say the flat-headed North African cats reminded me of the jaguarundi, or that I had some kind of epiphany when I went out to see, dutifully (but without a camera), the Sphinx. Or that I once spent an afternoon in a village near Luxor drinking cheap white wine with a Dutch girl who had a laugh, and hair, exactly like

Manette's. Or that I went with her to her hotel room and ran my hands down her shoulder blades, drew my fingers along the rim of her collarbone, like a fan of feathers skimming smooth bark. And that afterwards I listened to her tell me about Uxmal and Chichén, as if I'd never been there, I'd never heard of them, and everything she said, she did, even the way she smelled, was new and surprising.

I don't know if I could say all that; if it would be true, really.

I did see Manette again, once, briefly. I met her for breakfast at a Sanborn's near my hotel in the Colonia Centro. This was in 1992, when most of the earthquake damage had been repaired, although there were still a few empty lots here and there, boarded up with plywood. Another president was privatizing the banks; everyone was talking about a free trade agreement with the U.S. and Canada. The stock market had sailed up like a skyrocket, and my father had been calling me, telling me I should buy Telmex, Cifra, Cemex.

She wore a red suit that looked tight at the hips. Her hair was cut short, pulled back with a plastic headband. No, she hadn't painted anything in ages, there wasn't room in her apartment. Uwe had gone back to his first wife in Vienna. She had thought about moving to Houston, she said, but she was offered a job translating reports for the American Chamber of Commerce. It was fun, she said. It was nearby.

We ate hotcakes and drank coffee. She took out her compact and put on her lipstick. I lit a Marlboro. She'd been doing tai chi, on Saturdays, at the Casa de Cultura in Coyoacán. She'd been going to the Beverly Hills Workout at the Plaza Inn mall. The jaguarundi was in the zoo.

We split the bill. When I pushed back my chair, she touched my hand. "Where will you be going?" she said. She had fine lines around her eyes now.

"Chiapas," I said.

"You are?" Her voice was very soft. "Will you be back?"

"I don't know," I said.

It crossed my mind, as we said goodbye in the street, that she expected me to kiss her. But she was wearing heavy makeup and I didn't want to smudge it.

* * *

I was back in Mexico City the following week, and I went, to pass a few hours before my plane left, for old-time's sake, or for some reason I don't really want to admit to myself, to the Chapultepec zoo. I bought a hot dog and an orange soda and I walked along the winding paths shaded by eucalyptus and ancient *ahuehuetes*. The tiger I had fed so many years ago had died. The panda was on loan to a zoo in Washington, D.C., a little plaque said. I saw a gorilla with its tiny baby, a family of gibbons, a frantic chinchilla in a small cage. The zoo was nearly empty, but for a noisy group of schoolchildren in their navy blue uniforms. An old man sat on a bench, tossing popcorn to the pigeons.

I found the jaguarundi in a glassed-in cage, in a pavilion near the exit. It was sleeping, its head in its paws. Its fur was speckled with white. It looked thin. The cage had a backdrop painted to look like a jungle, with sloppy olive-green banana trees and a cloudless turquoise sky. I clapped my hands, but the jaguarundi didn't move. Its food dish was covered with flies. I clapped my hands again, louder this time, and its eyes flicked open. The jaguarundi looked at me without moving. Then it yawned and rolled over on its side.

I thought I might tap on the glass, call out its name. But for the life of me I couldn't remember what it was.

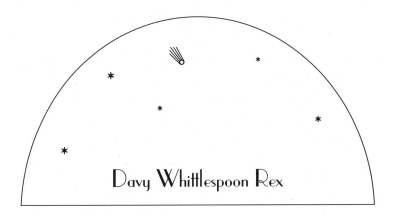

Davy Whittlespoon Rex

It was early September when Davy Whittlespoon came back from El Salvador, with a bright blotchy rash on his neck and a bag of *sorpresitas,* little surprises.

"I'd have brought you some *pollo campero,*" he told his mother, "but it would have smelled up the plane." Davy's laugh was a riffle, his palms moist with sweat.

His mother was sitting Indian-style on the sofa. She leaned forward with a grunt to set her drink on the coffee table. She narrowed her eyes at him and blew out a thick stream of menthol smoke.

"It's chicken," Davy said, still standing in the doorway. His black cowboy boots were creased with dust. "Like Kentucky Fried, but better."

His mother picked a fuzz nub off the arm of the sofa. She reached behind the lava lamp for the television remote control.

"*Pollo campero*'s sort of sweet maybe, not too spicy . . ." Davy squatted down and unzipped his duffel bag. He began to feel around the balled-up T-shirts and undershorts, jeans, the carefully folded newspapers, aftershave and antidandruff shampoo, for the plastic bag of tissue-wrapped *sorpresitas.* "They've got this secret recipe, supposedly," he said. "*Pollo campero*'s are everywhere in San Salvador. They're really clean, you know. Well-lit, fast, like Kentucky Fried."

"But better," his mother said. Her voice was sharp, bored. "What's wrong with your neck?"

"My neck?" Davy's hand fluttered to his Adam's apple.

"Looks like you got some mosquito hickeys." She aimed the control at the television like a gun.

"Ma." *Mosquito* had sounded like *mushkitter*. She had hiccuped. Davy stood up and pulled the door closed. "What are you drinking?"

"None of your goddammed business." His mother's eyes were glued to the screen, unblinking. An enormous black woman with an apple-shaped face was interviewing three white men. She was leaning forward towards one of them, moving her fists in circles, as if she were reeling in a line.

"Ma," Davy said.

"So how do you feel about that?" the black woman said.

"You do what you have to do," one of the white men said. This was the one who looked about sixty, who had milky blue eyes, who had his shirt unbuttoned down to his belt. He looked as if he felt blessed, flashing the gold in his teeth. He looked like Davy's father, Bart Whittlespoon.

"Ma." Davy's voice was low and clear as a cast-iron bell.

She drowned her cigarette in her drink, *fzzzzt*. Her face had turned the color of a boiled tomato.

This was a long time ago, when they were living in Southern California.

Her name was Estelle. She had the fattest thighs Davy had ever seen, and a platinum bouffant. Estelle preferred muumuus, in bright tropical colors. And plastic sandals that made a squishy *flurp-flurp* as she pushed their cart up and down the aisles of the supermarket. Otherwise, she mostly watched TV, sitting Indian-style on the sofa, her beautiful face stitched with pain. "Gotta cut the circulation," is how she explained it. She had a theory that if she could cut the circulation to her legs, she might redistribute the fat towards her upper body. She had tried grapefruit, yogurt, pills. She had tried lighting candles, and hoping for one of the Seven Miracles of Africa.

Davy clenched his eyes shut and stood very still. He listened to the commercial, something about a fabric softener. Then he lugged his duffel bag past the coffee table, through the narrow hallway, and into his room. There were fresh sheets on his bed, and the stucco walls smelled as if they had been wiped down with Lysol. On his bedside table was a cardboard frame that said "Kodak" in one corner. Estelle had scotch-taped in a photograph he'd not seen in years: Estelle and Davy with Mickey Mouse in front of Sleeping Beauty's castle. Davy had his arms locked around one of Mickey's legs, and the giant mouse's fat white gloves waved stiffly at the camera. And there was Tony Martínez, off to one side, in a Donald Duck hat, flashing the peace sign. Tony was Estelle's boyfriend, sometimes. Davy knelt down to look under the bed; his Heavy Metal collection was still there, an even stack wrapped in stolen Motel 6 towels to keep out the dust. Then, almost as an afterthought, Davy knocked the photograph face down.

He was unpacking when Estelle waddled into the doorway. She was wearing a low-cut parrot yellow muumuu. Her hair was very big, but slightly matted down on the right side. She leaned into the doorjamb and stared at Davy's arms, so sinewy, his steel watchband loose around his wrist. The veins in his arms were periwinkle blue.

"Okay," she said. Her voice was very loud. "So how's Bart the Old Fart? No, wait." She shuffled into the room. "No, don't tell me." She shoveled a pile of Davy's T-shirts and jeans onto his pillow and sat down, the bedsprings popping and groaning. "Did he send money?"

"Bart's fine," Davy said. "He didn't send money."

Bart Whittlespoon had been in the Merchant Marine, but he was retired now. He had a *ceviche* stand on the beach at La Libertad, about forty minutes out of San Salvador. Bart was not actually Davy's father, but Estelle had never found it convenient to let Davy or Bart know that. ("Strange to see a one-and-a-half-month premature baby that weighs 10 pounds," the doctor had said, peering at her from behind his clipboard. Estelle pulled up her hospital gown and slapped her thigh. "Healthy," she said. "Baby's goddammed healthy.")

"I'm totally outta dough," Estelle said. She had dark circles under her eyes. She lit a menthol cigarette and watched Davy thread his T-shirts onto hangers. She watched him tuck his sandals and tennis shoes into line on the closet shelf. "I don't even have money for supper."

Davy said, "Close your eyes, Ma." Estelle clenched her eyes shut, dragging on her cigarette. This was a joke between them; it meant he was going to put away his undershorts.

"No money, Davy boy."

Davy slammed the drawer shut with the heel of his boot. "Okay, Ma, you can open them now." He was taking small tissue-wrapped things out of a plastic bag. "I had to hide this one real well," he said, passing it to her. It was a boning knife with a wooden handle.

Estelle rubbed her finger along the handle where it said LA LIBERTAD, EL SALVADOR EN LA AMERICA CENTRAL in small, careful letters. "This is real nice," she said. The room had filled with curlicues of smoke. She drew the leather sheaf off the blade. "Good quality," she said. She touched its point with her fingertip. "Sharp." She slid the blade back into its sheaf. "You should carry this with you."

Davy smirked. "Right, Ma."

"No, really," Estelle said. She grabbed his wrist and pulled herself up with a jerk. "Here." She leaned into him unsteadily, her chin jabbing his shoulder, her breath rough and sugary. "Here." She jammed the knife into his back pocket. She slapped his buttock. "Just carry it here."

"Yow!" He yanked it out.

"I'm serious." Estelle fell back on the bed. Her face was wild. "My neighbor, Linda Hadley, she was mugged last week." Estelle was shouting. "I say they banged her too, but she won't admit it. And I had to spend my check to get new tires, after those kids from the other side of the freeway hacked 'em with a friggin' meat cleaver!"

"Really?" Davy pretended to sneeze. "They hacked your tires with a *meat cleaver?*"

"Yes!" Estelle screamed. "You just up and leave me, no calls, no nothin', and Bart—" She spat the name and let out a terrible sob. Her rib cage began to heave.

"Oh come on." Davy sat down and put his arm around his mother's shoulders. The fabric of her dress was a loose scratchy muslin. Her bouffant smelled strongly of strawberry perfume and menthol. "Come on," Davy whispered. A single teardrop slid to the tip of her nose, caught the low sun in the window, and sparkled. Estelle's shoulders were the size of a small girl's. She had a sprinkle of freckles across the bridge of her nose, like he did. There was something soft about her, like vanilla pudding. Davy pulled her head to his chest. "I wasn't gone that long," he said, stroking her cheek. His lips brushed her temple. "And Bart's just a dirty old man."

"Hey!" She swatted his hand. "Don't mess my hair." She flopped down on her back, as if the mere thought of Bart had exhausted her. She took a deep drag on her cigarette. Then she rested her hand with the cigarette over her heart. Her nails were painted the colors of the rainbow, her thumbs deep violet. She wore a pewter zodiac ring on her third finger. The smoke rushed up and dissolved into a cloud near the ceiling.

"Gotta put something on that rash, kiddo." Davy had his head between his knees, but their hips were still touching. "Alcohol," she said, reaching out to tickle the small of his back. "And I got some cortisone cream maybe."

Davy stepped over to the window and forced it open. The pane screeched against the groove, and in came a sound like the rush of the sea, one single enormous wave forever breaking, forever crashing. A riff hooked into Davy's mind, a line plucked out on a bass guitar, *Now that it's started, it'll never stop.* He set his elbows on the concrete ledge and gazed at the traffic, jammed to a crawl. The thin curtains billowed out in the soft breeze, which was tinged with salt, and now, in the last days of an Indian summer, a sour fishy seaweed smell. Just that morning, Davy had perched on the raw timber railing of Bart's *ceviche* stand, looking out over La Libertad. The beach was strewn with round black stones, dull under a nickel-colored dawn. Out where the Pacific rollers usually swelled and formed, there was only an indifferent churning, and the surf washed up weakly against the sand. The black stones were the size of sleeping dogs; wiry brown children scampered around them, hunting for crabs.

"So how's the war?" Estelle had propped herself up on one elbow. She dabbed her eyes with the corner of the pillowcase.

"It's happening," Davy said, still leaning out the window.

"You sure were cute as a bug," Estelle said. She had picked up the photograph. "I wouldn't of cracked a mirror myself." She took a deep drag on her cigarette and blew it back out through her teeth. " 'Member? This was right before you barfed on the Matterhorn."

"Teacup ride," Davy said. He scratched the back of his knee with the toe of his boot. "I threw up on Tony in the teacup ride." He was looking down at the empty parking lot. There was a ragged palm tree near the street. A woman stood waiting for her dog to finish peeing against its trunk.

"Well, d'ja see anything?" Estelle's voice was mottled.

Davy shrugged. His shoulders were thin as wishbones. "The kid who washes the dishes at Bart's place goes around saluting everybody." The little boy's name was Beto Beteta. He did a lot more than wash the dishes. Now Davy was rooting in his duffel bag, taking out small tissue-covered egg-shaped things.

"Looks like hell on TV," Estelle said.

"Yeah." The toes of Beto Beteta's left foot had been blown off. His left eye was sewn shut. Davy tore the tissue off one of the egg-shaped things. "This is a *sorpresita*," he said, brightening. He offered it to her. "They make them in a village called Ilobasco." It was a tiny hollow clay mango set on top of a silver-dollar-sized clay disk. He'd bought it at the airport. "Open it," he said.

Estelle lifted up the little mango. On the disk, fashioned in clay, was a very tiny, anatomically correct couple. Estelle held it out on the flat of her hand, her cigarette fuming between her fingers. "Well," she said, arching an eyebrow. "The missionary."

"Oh!" Davy's face flushed. He snatched it back. His tongue seemed to have stuck to the roof of his mouth. He wiped his palms on his hips. Quickly, he picked out another *sorpresita*, this one painted to look like the tip of a banana.

"Open this one, Ma."

The ash on Estelle's cigarette was dangerously long. She lifted the banana tip. There was a very tiny brown mother in a pink dress and turquoise shawl, washing a very tiny baby.

"Gee," Estelle said, holding it up. Her eyes glistened. "That's real sweet." And the ash fell on his bed.

* * *

They decided to hock the lava lamp and go to Pizza Hut. After that, Estelle said Tony could tide them over until her next check.

Davy planned to hock the TV. Davy had known Tony since Bakersfield, when they were still living in Bart Whittlespoon's apartment. Back then, when Tony came over to visit, Estelle would shutter the living room. That way, she said, the picture on the TV was clearer. Tony would sit for a while on the sofa, balancing a can of beer on his knee. He would talk back at the television, "You're a dog long in the chops, Bachelorette Number Three," or hum along with the tune to "Gilligan's Island." Sometimes Tony would ruffle Davy's hair and rub his back. Then Estelle would lock Davy in his room.

When Estelle moved in with her sister near San Jose, Tony showed up again, with a tattoo above his left bicep, a fire-spitting dragon coiled around the words PHUONG DONG LOVE YOU. He manned the rental counter at the Rollerama, where Estelle worked as a cashier. Then there was Reno, and Vacaville, when Tony said he was going to marry a girl named Debbie Sharon and Estelle punched out his front tooth; and six months in Eureka, where Tony had his false tooth put in. For a few weeks, when it was new, he could suck it out. Then he'd stick out his tongue with the tooth on it. "Chiclet!" he would say. "Got me a Chiclet!" This never made Davy laugh, not once.

There was a period when Tony drove a cement truck.

"So how's Tony?" Davy asked. They were pulling into the parking lot of Pizza Hut.

"Said he had to take something up the coast tonight." Estelle seemed distracted. "Got a bigger beer gut now. Few more white hairs." Suddenly Estelle craned her neck around to look at a brown pickup.

"Hey," Davy said. "Isn't that Tony's pickup?"

"Hell if it is." Estelle lit another cigarette, sucking hard. The tip crackled and glowed. "Hell if it is." She opened her purse, a shapeless green vinyl clutch, and took out a pint bottle of Kahlúa. She unscrewed it and passed it to him.

"Oh come on, Ma." Davy sounded very tired.

She threw back a slug, scrunching her nose as she swallowed.

"You're going to get sick, drinking on an empty stomach."

Estelle hissed, "Pizza Hut makes me sick."

Davy had parked the car, but the key was still in the ignition. "Well then," he said, "why don't we go to Kentucky Fried?" But Estelle was already out the door, her purse banging against her thigh, her muumuu flouncing in the breeze. Davy caught up with her just as she put her hand on the bar of the glass door. He closed his hands around her hand and made it into a tiny fist. Estelle's eyes were black. The zodiac ring bit into his flesh. "Please," he said. He had broken out in a heavy sweat. Her jaw clamped shut. Her eyes constricted to steely points.

They walked into the restaurant arm in arm. In the fluorescent light, her muumuu was school-bus yellow, her platinum bouffant just another shade of bottle blonde. Davy ordered a medium pineapple and ham pizza and two large Cokes. At the far table in the corner, they could see the back of Tony's head. He had a bald spot about the size of a baseball, and he was wearing a greasy looking jeans jacket. He was sitting with a blonde girl who had a grown-out shag haircut and a constellation of scabs on her chin. She leaned forward over their pizza and whispered something, and Tony laughed, a hoarse donkey *haw-haw*. Estelle shuffled over to sit at a booth on the other side of the empty restaurant, near the cash registers. Davy took his change without counting it and walked towards his mother, scuffing his boots along the tiles, stuffing the coins into his front pocket. The girl's eyebrows had been plucked to pencil lines. Very slowly, she held a triangle of pizza to her mouth and touched it with the tip of her tongue. She was staring at Davy's crotch.

"Sir!" It was the manager, who had taken their order. "I see you have a knife!" He had called it out softly, like a question. He was wearing a white shirt and a brown polyester necktie with a clip on it.

Davy spun around on one heel. He yanked the tail of his shirt out to hide the handle. He was about to say something, but Estelle yelled, "How's he supposed to cut the pizza?"

"Sir." The manager's face seemed to unravel. He crossed his arms over his chest. Just then a stout man in a double-breasted navy blazer and brass-rimmed sunglasses pushed open the door. He was holding the hand of a tiny girl. She was wearing ballerina slippers, blue jeans, and a primrose pink leotard. She pranced in and ran up to the register.

"What'll you have, Princess?" The stout man scanned the menu board. He slipped his sunglasses in his jacket pocket. Arms akimbo, he smiled agreeably at the manager. "This is all new for us," he said.

"Take your time, sir." The manager had a sallow complexion and a double chin. He had his eye on Davy and Estelle. Estelle was swigging the last of the Kahlúa.

"Extra gigantic pepperoni with triple cheese!" the girl cried out in a doll-like voice. She put her hands on the counter and bent her knees in a lazy plié.

"Anything to drink, sir?"

"Gallon o' Lysol," Estelle muttered under her breath. She crushed her empty packet of menthols into a ball. "Davy here'll toss a match."

"Extra gigantic Coca-Cola!" The girl was hopping, kicking her leg out. The man pulled her firmly towards his waist. "That's enough, Princess. Settle down now." And to the manager: "Two large Cokes."

Tony still had not turned around. Every once in a while his head bobbed up and down and he let out a ridiculous *haw-haw*. Estelle's lips were pursed tightly together. Davy mopped his forehead with a paper napkin. The man and the little girl sat down two tables away from Estelle and Davy. The manager brought out their ham and pineapple pizza and Cokes.

From across the restaurant, Tony burst out with a glorious braying *haw-haw*. Estelle began to shake red pepper flakes onto her pizza, furiously.

"Mom never lets me eat pizza," the little girl said to the man. "Nothing with—" She hesitated. "Poly-un-sat-ur-rated fats." She slurped her Coke. Her white-blonde hair was pulled back with a broad pink band, and her skin glowed. "Just veggie burgers and salads 'n stuff," she said with disgust.

"You mean *saturated* fats," the man said. He rubbed his eyes, and then blinked at the girl, as if he had trouble believing she were really his.

"And Coca-Cola," she said very seriously, "Never! I *never* get to have Coca-Cola!"

Suddenly Estelle let out a massive belch. The little girl twisted around and stared, pale and shocked. Davy buried his face in his napkin and pushed the heels of his palms into the bone around his eyes. He had tried arguing; Heavy Metal. He had tried living with Bart. He began to see stars.

"Hey, Tony," she bellowed, "what's she charging you?" Tony jackknifed in his seat. His mouth hung open. "Lemme guess!" Estelle slammed her fist on the table and the shaker of red hot pepper flakes clattered to the floor.

And galaxies. They orbited each other rapidly, in jagged elipses. They formed surprising configurations.

* * *

The clouds were angry welts on a yellow sky. A line of palm trees stood between the parking lot and a high-rise office building. They seemed to bend in the breeze, to hear.

"You shouldn't be seeing this," Davy said gently.

The little girl was standing just outside the glass door, holding the man's navy blazer over her arm. One sleeve dragged on the ground. Davy held the door open for her.

"What?" She darted her head around him, trying to see, to follow what they were saying. They were yelling. The manager was shaking his fist at Estelle. The blonde girl was shouting, "Fuck! Fuck!" over and over again, to no one in particular. The stout man was bending over Tony, who lay on his back next to a silver Mercedes coupe that was smeared with blood.

Davy took the little girl's hand and led her back inside the restaurant. He bought her an ice cream sundae. A slack-faced boy in a cap took the order.

"You're short a penny," the boy said.

"It's all I've got," Davy said. "Can't you give me a break?"

"You're short a penny," the boy said, in exactly the same tone of voice.

The little girl dug into her jeans pocket and slapped a coin on the counter.

"Thanks," Davy said.

"You're welcome," she said.

Davy steered her to a table next to the window. She began to spoon the chopped nuts over to one side of the dish. She looked at his neck, quickly. Then she stirred the nuts into a puddle of vanilla on the side.

"My name is Sophie Nix," she said, locking her eyes to his. "What's yours?"

"Is that Sophie with a 'ph' and Nix with an 'x'?" Davy asked.

"What?"

Davy glanced out the window. The clouds had turned the color of ashes.

"Does your sister know that man?"

"She's not my sister." Davy began to chew his thumbnail.

The girl poked the cherry into the whipped cream with her pinky. She started to fold the vanilla into the chocolate, the whipped cream into the vanilla. "How come she got so mad at him?"

" 'Cause." Davy raked his fingers through his hair. Then he rested his elbow on the table and began to chew his thumbnail again.

The girl cocked her head, looking at Davy carefully. "Well I think you look like that man."

"Who?"

"That man that got hurt!" she said, impatiently. "You walk the same way," she said. She shimmied her shoulders and thrust out her chin. "You have the same face."

Davy's thumbnail was bitten to the quick. "You know what?" he said. He took a paper napkin out of the dispenser and squeezed it around his finger. "I know a little boy about your age. He's called Baby. Know why?"

The girl shook her head violently.

" 'Cause his real name is Beto Beteta. B.B. for Beto Beteta. But in Spanish you say 'B.B.' like *bebe,* which means 'baby.' "

The girl buried her spoon in the sundae. She sat up very straight and clasped her hands together on the table.

Davy said, "Baby knows how to do lots of things. He can catch crabs. He can tie all kinds of knots. He can make *ceviche*. You know what *ceviche* is?" Her eyes darted about the empty restaurant, towards the window. The sharp wail of sirens had begun, several blocks away.

"It's a cocktail made of raw fish," Davy said. The girl shrank in her seat. "But you marinate it in lime juice, and that cooks it. It's real good." She narrowed her eyes at him, but Davy wasn't looking at her anymore. "And Baby knows how to wash clothes, and iron shirts. He can sweep the floor, and wipe down the sinks. He makes necklaces out of tiny shells and shark bones. And he sells them—" The sirens

were coming in deafening waves. He was going to say, To the jour-
nalists who come out to watch the sun sink into the ocean like a fist.
Or a boiled tomato. A blob in the lava lamp.

An ambulance barrelled into the parking lot.

Just that morning, Beto Beteta was waving a rag at him from the
stoop by the kitchen. Davy was in the back of Bart Whittlespoon's
jeep, the duffel bag propped on the front seat like a corpse. Then the
jeep pulled out, spewing up an immense cloud of dust. Now Davy
could only see the road in front of him, but very clearly: the back
of Bart's leathery neck, the palms and jacarandas laden with vines,
with brilliant bougainvillea, plum, parrot yellow. Sky blue. And sleek
ebony birds hopping at the edge of the highway.

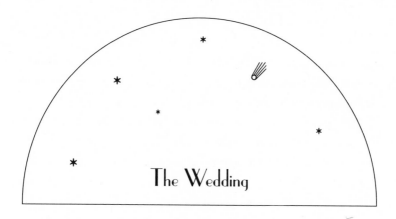

The Wedding

Lola makes tiny circling motions around her eyes, the crow's-feet, and across the bridge of her nose, where she has a wrinkle so sharp it might be the mark of a hatchet. She faces the mirror square on and bares her teeth. They have fine coffee-colored fissures, she knows, but her cataracts have spread, and her teeth might as well be seed pearls, round-edged and polished. Lola squints (an old exercise), as if through the haze of her lashes and clouds on her eyes she might catch a glimpse of herself as she once was. She touches her fingertips to her jowls. The loose skin is moist and papery, but she can feel the bone, still thick and hard.

It is early afternoon on an April Saturday. Lola has missed the Mass. Now she tucks a stray strand of white hair behind her ear, and then she pinches the lobe just below her earring. "*Vieja tonta,*" Stupid old fool, she hisses at the vanity mirror. Her lobe smarts, but it remains unchanged, bloodless. The earring looks like a solid teardrop.

The Mass was the wedding of her granddaughter Araceli Sánchez and Santiago Grimm, a tall sandy-haired boy whom Lola has never heard mumble more than one or two words. She cannot decide whether Santiago is timid and perhaps (the slackness in his jaw suggests it) stupid, or whether he is quite capable of behaving in an entirely different fashion when not in her presence. Lola has tried to imagine Santiago in black leather trousers, playing "air guitar," like an American rock star on MTV, the television station Araceli watches. MTV goes on and on, song after song, crazy screaming and electric guitars that sound like a band of bagpipers run amok.

In fact, Santiago wears penny loafers and khaki pants, and when absolutely necessary, a sloppily knotted silk tie.

Now Lola runs her fingertips down her neck and she imagines Santiago in a white terrycloth robe, smiling at Araceli from the balcony of their hotel room. Araceli and Santiago will honeymoon at a golf and tennis resort on Maui. His family owns the chain of Grimm department stores. Grimm department stores are absolutely everywhere in Mexico City. Lola fingers her earring. She thinks about the Grimm where she bought it the week before. There was a brown patent-leather clutch on sale which she wanted to buy. But why, she asks the mirror, accumulate things only to leave them to her heirs, practically new, so soon? Araceli would have no use for an old lady's purse. And Carmen, Lola's daughter, would say brown patent leather was *naca*, something a military officer's mistress or a secretary might want. Better to save the money; one always has use for cash.

Yet why, Lola realizes, should Carmen, or for that matter Araceli, now that she has married Santiago Grimm, care one whit for the pathetic sums she expects to leave them? Carmen would scold Araceli, "You should pray for your Gramma Lola. Look what she left you— nothing? Five million pesos and some jewelry. Well, it's something. It's what she had."

Why did Lola miss the Mass? She cannot trust herself to decide. She had her bath at nine-thirty, as usual, her breakfast brought to her at ten: a sweet roll buttered to look like a shell, and a glass of orange juice with (just a splash of) tequila. She pulled on her pink American jogging outfit and tennis shoes, the ones Carmen brought her from a shopping trip to Houston. She tucked her hair into a flowered cotton scarf and took out Buni, her miniature poodle, for his morning trot around the block. It was warm for an April morning. The bougainvillea hanging over the garden walls on her street seemed tired, their pastel blossoms shriveled. Halfway around, Lola had to tug Buni along by his leash, and a few meters from home, at the clump of wilted red amaryllis, Buni stopped and sat back on his haunches, panting heavily. "Bunito," Lola crooned, "come with Mama," and she yanked his leash. His toenails scratched against the pavement, and for a brief moment his eyes bugged out.

When she came home, Buni padded into the kitchen for his water and then lay flat out on the tiles, his belly to the cold. Lola stretched out on her bed, just for a little rest before her hair appointment. Her hair would be washed and set with gel, and then teased. It would be large and waved and sprayed just so, which would take away, if not the years, at least some measure of the terrible harshness in her face. But she fell into a reverie that was like a tepid bath, the images in her mind neither the cold machinations of calculation nor the fevers of sleep. She was at her own wedding, she was nineteen years old again, the chestnut-haired girl everyone called *chula* and *linda* and *guapa*. Her skin was firm and olive-pink, her lips red without lipstick, and the organ hummed out something like children whispering, or pine needles brustling in a soft wind. The dead were young again, Mother, Father with his salt-and-pepper mustache, all the aunts and uncles, cousins, and school friends. La nana Martita with her enormous belly and Indian braids; Gramma Luz María, wearing her beady grin and her Chinese silk shawl. Lola's dress was a snowy velvet. She could even feel the line of velvet-colored buttons prickling her spine . . .

It wasn't that; the sheets were twisted, crumpled under her sweating back. Lola let out a deep sigh. She could hear Buni's paws on the tiles in the hallway, his tag clinking against his collar. It was getting late, and she would have to dress for her hair appointment, call the driver on the intercom, tell him to take out the car. But she fell into her thoughts again, diving down to where the coolest, sweetest waters swirled around and around, to where tallow church candles flickered in the thin city air. The chapel was suffused with a rich perfume of incense and roses. The groom was her dead husband, he was Carmen's husband, he was Santiago, sandy-haired, in a loose black and gray striped cravat. His eyes searched her crown, the line of her chin, the tight black curls on her temples, *chula, divina,* and he grasped her hands, smooth and dewy, in his. She clenched her fists, and she held a bouquet of pink roses and baby's breath. Then she held a child, small and panting, its tiny arms winding around her neck. Then it was something jumpy and furry: Buni licking her face.

Lola tossed the dog to the floor and sat up on the bed. She felt as if her head were in a plastic bag, under water. She checked her watch: the Mass would start in less than five minutes. No time to have her hair done. No time to repair her nails. She had a sudden sinking feeling, as if there were a small pile of stones in her stomach. She drew the back of her hand across her forehead to calm herself. *Ni modo,* no matter.

* * *

Lola pulls out a green eye pencil, and with a shaky hand, begins to draw along one lid. She realizes, suddenly, that Carmen will disapprove of green eye pencil. Carmen will hate the perfume that smells of gardenias, just as she would hate the brown patent-leather clutch from Grimm's that would have gone so well with the beige tea-length chiffon dress, the dress Lola bought especially for this wedding, the very day after Santiago asked Carmen's husband for permission. Lola bought it at Grimm's, and not on sale. The dress is draped across a chair by the window. Lola can see the dress in the vanity mirror; it has a slight shine to it. She considers this shine for a moment. She decides the dress must have a high polyester content.

"*Vieja tonta,*" she says to the mirror. She gathers her thin white hair into a rubber band to make a bun, but the front strands are too short. She shouts for her maid to bring her a box of bobby pins, but "*Señora,*" the teenage voice floats up from the stairwell, "*no hay,*" there aren't any. Now Lola must paste her hair down with a gel that gives it a queer bluish-green cast.

She can already hear her daughter, disappointed that she missed Araceli's and Santiago's Mass. "Mama!" Carmen would rasp, her voice hoarse from years of smoking. She would clasp Lola's arm just above her elbow, as if it were a young girl's wrist. (Carmen's nails would be perfect, polished vermilion, very long.) "Mama! How can you show up to Araceli's wedding so *naca?*" Carmen would knit her brow at the uneven green lines penciled across Lola's eyelids. She would roll her eyes at Lola's hair. "I should have taken you to the beauty parlor myself. Oh God." Carmen would rattle around in her purse for a cigarette, but then she would think better of it. She would put her hand to her décolletage, running a palm across her Virgin of Guadalupe medal in a nervous back-and-forth.

Lola is ready. She takes each step carefully, leaning against the rail, reminding herself that her bones are fragile. She imagines falling and breaking her hip, or her arm. She might crack her head. She might be found in a pool of dried blood, hours later, by her maid. She might die—or worse: she could be kept alive, unconscious, for months on an artificial respirator, force-fed glucose solution through a yellow plastic tube up her nose. Carmen and Araceli would have to come to the hospital every day and exercise her elbows, her wrists, to keep them from clenching into strange twisted positions. (But Araceli would be on Maui with Santiago, learning to surf. Carmen would need to go to Houston with her husband.) Lola pats her hair. It lies flat against her skull, and it feels stiff and dry.

Her driver, as usual, is inscrutable as he opens the back of the Ford sedan for her. He mutters, "*Tardes,*" Afternoon, under his breath. Lola settles onto the buttery leather seat and smooths her dress with her palms. Her hands are knobby with arthritis, and she has not repaired the chipped pink polish. Her diamond ring sparkles in the sunlight. It is the yellow of very weak camomile tea. Lola tells the driver to take her directly to Carmen's house. He grunts as he turns the key in the ignition.

The wedding party will be a lunch in Carmen's garden. Carmen has not been able to talk about anything else for weeks. She has contracted Arnaud-Ortiz, the most expensive caterer in Mexico City. She has hired an enormous white tent, with a crystal chandelier hanging down from the gathered center, and tables with folding chairs, and linen chair-covers with oversized bows on the back (as shown in the Martha Stewart coffee table book *Weddings*). And Carmen has rented tablecloths with pink and red cabbage roses on a beige background, although Araceli wanted the tablecloths with lavender wildflowers. (Araceli insisted that lavender would look prettier against the ivy-covered walls by the cabaña. Cabbage roses, she said, were "old ladyish.") White-gloved waiters will pass platters of *crepas de cuitlacoche,* and then chicken with *axiote* in banana leaves. For the cake, a construction of Amaretto-soaked sponge, meringue, shredded coconut, and butter-cream frosting. Araceli had wanted to release 1,994 pink and white balloons, the same number as the year, something she said was (Lola cannot remember which) good luck or the latest fashion with her friends. Lola wonders if Carmen has been able to find enough tanks of helium for this purpose.

The swimming pool will be decorated with specially made floating baskets of calla lilies and votive candles, to be lit at sundown. Lola winces and rubs her hands together as she remembers how furious Araceli was about this arrangement. At last Sunday lunch Araceli nearly shouted when she said, "But Mama, there won't be any room to dance if we don't cover the pool!" Araceli had insisted that the pool could be covered with thick sheets of plywood and anchored somehow. "At Malú's and George's wedding they covered the pool." Araceli's eyes teared up with frustration. "They even put three tables of ten people on top of it!"

Lola had brightened at the idea of such ingenuity. She laid down her fork and said, "But imagine."

Carmen snapped, "Well, yes. Imagine. At Inés' and Chucho's wedding, when people started dancing, the plywood cracked apart and half the wedding party—including Inés—fell into the pool."

"Poor Inés," Lola said.

"Yes," said Carmen, staring pointedly at Araceli, "Poor Inés."

Lola had no idea who any of these people were.

Lola's car pulls up to Carmen's house. The street is empty but for the caterer's truck and a beat-up looking Volkswagen. For a moment the Volkswagen worries her. She knows of two people who know people who were at a wedding taken over by masked robbers. They had come in before the party started (apparently in cahoots with the waiters) and hidden behind some bushes. When all the guests were seated, the thieves jumped out, waving machine guns. Lola twists her diamond ring around her finger once, twice, and tries to think what she should do. When the thieves begin making the rounds of the tables nearest the bushes, she might drop her ring into the sauce boat. She might hide under the table and breathe very carefully. She has a friend whose husband nearly lost an eye after he was pistol-whipped in a restaurant.

She decides the Volkswagen belongs to one of the waiters. The driver holds open her door. Over the wall, on the other side of the house, she spies a white balloon caught in the branches of a giant jacaranda tree. Carmen's maid comes to the front gate. Her face is round and blank. "Señora," she says in a harried voice, "there's nobody here yet." A little girl, who is perhaps three, although, Lola judges, perhaps four or even five, clings shyly to her mother's apron. She is wearing a frilly red jumper and cheap black Mary Janes without socks. The maid wipes her hands on her apron and shoos the child towards the side yard, the laundry patio.

On her way to the garden Lola walks through the living room. Carmen has clustered family photographs in antique silver frames on the mantel, on side tables, and in half a dozen unlikely niches. Lola stops to review the photographs on the mantel. She cannot see the detail, but she knows that this one is of Carmen's wedding, and this one a candid shot of Carmen leaning over to kiss someone, her mantilla submerged in a sea of heads. Lola is holding up the dirtied tip of Carmen's train. Lola's eyes have deep shadows. She looks puffy, blanched, as if the weight of the organdy were simply much too much. And there is Lola sitting on the sofa, her skirt hiked up, holding baby Araceli. The baby's face is beet red. Lola's skirt is covered with large purple polka dots, and her hair has begun to grow out white. Such an unattractive photograph, Lola thinks. She has asked Carmen to put it away, how many times? She picks up the frame and gingerly sets it face down behind the others, Carmen and her husband on his sailboat, Araceli and Santiago splashing each other in the swimming pool, and a group photograph of the family from a ski vacation ten years ago: Lola's cheeks have hollowed, and she has developed a wattle under her chin.

She says out loud, to no one in particular, to the photographs, "I never thought I would see the wedding of my granddaughter." She cups her palm over her mouth. But I am dying in stages, she thinks. They are watching me die.

On the baby grand piano, next to a blue and white Talavera bowl of sachet, there is another little forest of frames. Carmen and Araceli at Disneyland, Araceli and her cousins at St. Peter's in Rome (the white and glass box of the Popemobile at the far corner), and a yellowed formal portrait of Gramma Luz María. She stands stiffly in a dark dress with an exaggerated bustle. Her face is unsmiling, but Lola remembers her as an animated person, someone who loved to tell about the time Zapata's soldiers broke into her father's cellar and smashed his bottles of French champagne with their machete handles.

"You will be seventy before you know it," Gramma Luz María had cackled at Lola, the very morning of the day she died. Lola was twenty then, six months married. Gramma Luz María's voice was sharp and small. "You will be seventy faster than a pistol shot."

It was true, the truest thing Lola can think of ever having been told in her life. But she would never say anything like that to Araceli. Araceli would roll her eyes and say, "Oh, Gramma. God."

Lola steps out into the garden and it is, indeed, as beautiful as Carmen had planned it. The tent is a soft clean white, and the cabbage rose tablecloths spring-like and pretty. The pool sparkles turquoise, and the baskets of calla lilies float lazily around the tiled steps at the shallow end. There is a not-unpleasant smell of freshly mown grass, and from the cabaña the gentle clink of glasses and bottles as the waiters set up the bar. The maid's little girl has found a half-filled balloon, and she tosses it up into the air and then catches it as it slowly arcs back down again. Lola watches the child skip around the garden, weaving around the edges of the tent and tables, and she is reminded of Carmen, playing with an inflated ball painted with cartoon dolphins on the sand in Acapulco. And of Araceli, how she would skip around this very garden, such a short time ago, so happy with her American Barbie dolls. And of herself, with a hoop and a stick and dusty black lace-up boots.

Lola spots a waiter walking towards the house from the cabaña. She waves and calls out, "Boy! A Cuba libre!" She sits down at a table on the edge of the tent by the pool, and he brings the rum and cola to her immediately, on a silver tray. She takes a greedy swallow, surprised at how thirsty she is. Beads of water form on the glass, and she touches her forehead with the coolness of it. It really is a gorgeous afternoon. She admires the centerpiece of flowers Carmen has chosen: pink and white rosebuds with baby's breath. She closes her eyes and drinks in their smoothness, this essence, she decides, of April. She takes a sip of her drink. A flash of red: the maid's child is tapping her balloon across the lawn towards the swimming pool. The sky is very nearly the blue of the pool, and the clouds are high, moving quickly. They look like cotton puffs, or perhaps half-filled white balloons.

Lola raises her glass to her lips again and winces. How she must look, she thinks, sitting all alone, her wrinkled lips pursed around the lip of this glass. *La naca vieja,* with her polyester dress, her jowls, her hair plastered into a sad little bun. She imagines that Araceli will have a baby that looks just like Santiago and it will scream whenever she tries to kiss it. The white balloon blows out over the pool, and with a soft *sploosh* the child falls into the deep end.

For a moment Lola only registers this: that the pool is shimmering crazily, that the baskets of calla lilies have begun to toss, and that something red is sinking, slowly. Lola throws her drink on the table and shoves back her chair, and suddenly she is running across the grass faster than she can remember running in years, and years. She is aware of the riffle of the jacaranda's leaves, of the smell of yellow-green grass cuttings, of a great empty space beneath her rib cage. As she slips off her shoes and curls her toes around the cement rim of the deep end, Lola thinks, Oh! She sucks in her breath and crouches forward, towards the undulating red blur, the crazy shimmering blue. Oh!

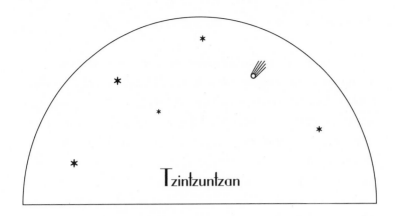

Tzintzuntzan

Adios Mama Carlota
Adios mi tierno amor
Se fueron los franceses
¿Quién quiere el emperador?
  Popular Mexican song, 1866

The ficus trees were shivering in their clay pots. The hummingbird had not come. From her bedroom, Charlotte could hear Benita, the cook, washing the dishes downstairs. She heard a thud, crash, and the sound of water rushing over the side of the sink. "*¡Ay, mierditas!*" Benita swore rapid-fire. "*¡Tremenda cagada!*"

The phone began to ring, an insistent satanic chirping. It would be Max, but Charlotte had no intention of picking it up. "*¡Se le metió el demonio!*" Benita's voice was high, bird-like. "*¡Está chingado!*" There were three high-pitched splinters, as if Benita had thrown bits of crockery against the wall.

Charlotte splayed her toes, her fingers. She arched her back. She pulled the duvet over her head and curled up in the fetal position. Now Benita was calling for her, "*¡Señora! ¡Señora! ¡Venga para acá!*" Come here!

* * *

The hummingbird had not come, but the gas truck did; it came at seven that morning, screeching its way into the narrow cobblestone street, then sputtering like a dying mammoth. It disgorged the month's supply of propane, and when it pulled out, it shredded the neighbor's red Volkswagen bug. The driver's assistant, who had been waving and pounding the flank of the truck, whistling out his directions, thought this was the funniest thing he'd seen since the Saturday matinee. He'd hopped up into the cab with a smile as large as a watermelon wedge.

Benita was calling for her, "*¡Señora! ¡Señora! ¡El teléfono! ¡Es el Señor Max!*"

Charlotte could hear the distant rumbling, even through the down-filled duvet. The sky would be gray mud. She clamped a pillow over her head. It smelled of bleach. The little red Volkswagen was still parked there under her window, smashed and nicked, gunmetal gray through its gashes.

Benita was pounding on her bedroom door.

"*¡Señora! ¡El teléfono! ¡Es para usted!*"

Charlotte screamed.

Charlotte's friend was named Karlota. K-K-K-Karlota. Children should be given names that start with hard consonants: Kristin, Kathryn, Karlota. Charlotte had read that somewhere. She thought of her own name: Charlotte. Sharon, Cheryl, Shelley. Puffball names, for nice American girls with pink barrettes and a little milk mustache on their upper lip.

"You should go to Veracruz." That's what Karlota said. Karlota had a job with a French investment bank. Karlota did something with bonds, on the telephone. Charlotte had seen her office once. It was in the nightclub district, in a glass-front high-rise. Karlota's desk was strewn with notepads, booklets, papers, faxes, all of them covered with typed and scribbled numbers. Her computer sat on a low table to the side, and its screen glowed green, more numbers, hundreds, thousands of billions.

Karlota said she had a view of the volcanoes. But the day Charlotte was there, clouds draped over the foothills like a shroud.

"Veracruz is cool," Karlota said. "Don't wait around for Max, just go there. Check it out."

"Oh, come with me." Charlotte had stood there with her feet pigeoned in, twisting a strand of her hair. "Please."

"Got the Telmex deal coming up."

Charlotte began to sob. Karlota grabbed Charlotte's shoulders to steady her. But then her face softened and she pulled Charlotte to her chest, drawing her fingers through Charlotte's hair, so silk smooth from scalp to tip, stroking down between her shoulder blades, so narrow. Charlotte's tears stained Karlota's turquoise blouse green, her hair tangled in Karlota's pearls, in Karlota's bracelet of gold-plate sun disks. Karlota whispered in her ear, "It'll be okay, come on," her breath cold coffee, but her throat jasmine lime, the sun.

Karlota slid open her desk drawer. A tissue ripped against cardboard. "So let's grab lunch, huh?" She dabbed at Charlotte's cheeks, rough on the soft skin under the eyes. "Where ya wanna go?"

* * *

The hummingbird had not come. He had come every day that week, his thumb-sized body glinting green-black in the sun, wings a blur as he hovered around the ficus trees, nipping at the geraniums, the bell-like fuchsia blossoms, the dwarf orange. Charlotte pressed her palms down on the pillow, flattening her nose against the mattress. Outside her window, the cobblestones were littered with bougainvillea blossoms, livid purple, red, white. A jacaranda branch lay like a severed arm, glistening under the streetlight.

And the ruined Volkswagen.

Benita had stopped pounding.

"*¡Le digo al Señor ¿qué?!*" What will I tell your husband? "*¿Que está enferma?*" That you are sick?

Charlotte's hair slid along the underside of the duvet, silk on damask. Right here, right now, the small of her back, the backs of her ears, crooks of her elbows: an all-over, perfectly even gooseflesh warm.

"*¡Ay, mierditas!*" And Charlotte heard the sound of hooves clapping down the wooden stairs.

∗ ∗ ∗

So they had gone to eat where Karlota always ate, a French restaurant so small it had only six tables. It was wedged behind a copy shop, lit with long fluorescent rods, and it smelled less of bacon and gruyère than of toner and of something hot and magnetic.

"You should go to Veracruz." That's what Karlota said, her mouth full of chicken. "Travel," she mumbled. "Go 'way." Chewing and swallowing and cutting. Stabbing with the tines of her fork. Karlota wore Chanel No. 5, or was it Joy de Patou? Daubed on her wrists, on her throat, and Charlotte wanted to reach across the table and press a finger there, under the top button of her V-neck blouse, warm and dark. Karlota's skin was bronze, her eyes gray-black dyed lashes, lips the color of swollen nipples. "The Gulf!" Karlota sliced her chicken. "The sun!"

Charlotte threw back her glass of Pernod. She thought of Max, and of the little moles on his back changing color, changing shape. When they went to the house in Cuernavaca, Charlotte slathered his shoulders with sunblock. She imagined her hand rubbing the white cream through his body hair, thick and curly brown; she felt her face drain parchment, her lips blister cochineal. "But Karlota," she said. The veins on her temples throbbed. "It's the rainy season."

"But Charlotte. So Fucking What?"

* * *

Wrap a dried hummingbird in silk and carry it in your pocket. That's what Benita said. *Así, México le querrá más.* That way Mexico will treat you better. *Así, el Señor Max le querrá más.* But Charlotte had given a dinner party for Karlota. The Chippendale table had been polished with lemon wax, the Empire sideboard rubbed with thick slices of ripe coconut. In the hallway by the stairs, Charlotte had arranged hawaiianas, birds of paradise, and blue irises in a waist-high Puebla ginger jar. Benita set out votive candles, polished the silver, and began cooking in the early morning. There would be twelve in all: Charlotte, Max, Karlota, Karlota's boss (Max's childhood friend), some of Max's people, some of Karlota's people, someone from the Embassy.

By late afternoon Benita was crying, her left cheek dangerously swollen. Charlotte called Benita's dentist and a taxi. She put the rack of veal in the oven, she made the *buerre blanc au romarin.* She whipped the cream for the chocolate torte. Two hours later Benita was back, a bloody rag pressed to her mouth. Charlotte touched the rag, and a thick rivulet of blood ran down over Benita's chin.

It dripped on the carpet, the cream-colored shag.

* * *

"*¡Es el Señor Max! ¡Otra vez!*" Again! Charlotte felt her breath whiffle against the sheet, light and hot. She squeezed shut her eyes and saw Benita's black braids, writhing on her back like snakes. She saw her peasant blouse with the red check ruffles, her brown fist smashing the door.

"*¡Es el Señor Max! ¡Por teléfono!*"

* * *

Like a sleepwalker, Charlotte had packed her briefcase for Veracruz. She had taken a taxi to the train station and bought a first-class ticket. She sat in her seat, staring out the window, hour after hour, hills and rows of corn and hills and gunpowder sky. She arrived in Veracruz near midnight, the summer sky now velvet black, dreamy white around the edges from the lights of the city. The Gulf was an angry cauldron, and everywhere, the smell of salt water and seaweed, seagull droppings and fungus. She walked along the *malecón,* on one side the dark water shimmering, licking up against the concrete, and on the other shuttered stalls and the lobbies of cheap hotels, bright glowing boxes.

At last she came to the plaza, where colored lights were strung up and a lone marimba band still played, dopey and loud. Most of the tables under the porticos were empty, but scattered knots of sailors hunched over backgammon and dominoes, and a hugely fat man sat by himself, using a long spoon to fish for something in a soda glass filled with tomato sauce. An Indian dressed in loose white cotton wound his way among the sailors, holding out an open box of cigars, bouncing the marionettes that dangled from his arm.

Charlotte patted her briefcase.

She would sit for a while, drink in the thick bitter air, order a beer and a *vuelve a la vida,* with rills of Tabasco sauce and lime. The fat man put his lips around the spoon and rolled his eyes. The Indian's eyes were widening, black: Charlotte would buy a Big Fat Cigar. Light it up and smoke it. Suddenly the marimba player threw his chin up towards the colored bulbs and hit the same notes again and again, *donk, donk, donk.* His partner shook the maracas with a frenzy, and it was over. A crack of thunder, the air became sea.

* * *

Tzintzuntzan, that's what Benita called the hummingbird. Tzintzuntzan, a Tarascan city on the shore of Lake Pátzcuaro. Charlotte had
always meant to go there, to organize something with Max, take her
old German camera, the one that was so small yet so heavy, that
made a *scht-klick* so precise Max would laugh and say, "And *we* lost
the war?"

There would be a field of gray rubble mounds, pyramids baking
under an indifferent sky. Then rain clouds would blow across the lake,
immense, rippling silver. Long grasses would sprout in the patter,
covering the mounds like a soft green fur, and bougainvilleas, and
brilliant pink and yellow wildflowers. Then in the white of a cool
mist hummingbirds would dart about, the air filling with their gentle
phwhirr phwhirr. The sky would clear, Prussian blue. A wide stairway
with ramps faced the lake.

"Do I love you?" Charlotte would ask, a question that would not
need to be answered.

Max sat at the top of the stairs, fiddling with the camera.

"Ready." He held out the camera. "Take my picture." He wore
knee-length khaki shorts and Swiss hiking boots. His golf hat was
bright white. He stood up and looked out at the lake, arms akimbo,
squinting.

"Max, I don't remember that golf hat."

Max turned around, but his face was gone. *Phwirr.* There was a
terrible buzzing. "*¡Carajo!*" Benita was stamping through the foyer.
"*¡Maldito cabrón!*" She slammed the foyer door, stalked through the
patio towards the garage, to the street. *Buzz buzz buzzzz.*

"*¡Voy!*" I'm coming!

It was the neighbor, a thin woman with frizzed hair and skin the
color of watered molasses. She was shouting. "*¿Cómo que no lo vieron?*"
How could you not have seen it? "*¿Cómo que no llamaran a la policia?*"

How could you not have called the police? The woman was hysterical. "How can you tell me, to my face, that you do not know who did this to my car? You think I have money? I don't have money! Your *patrona* has a big black Ford Grand Marquis! She has a banker for a husband! What do I have? A Mexican history teacher! Who knows all about things like the Gadsden Purchase!"

Her name was Margarita Maza. "A crummy little Volkswagen bug! That's all I have! Smashed! In front of your house! Where is the Señora Charlotte? I want to talk to the Señora Charlotte!"

"*Es que está enferma la señora.*" The señora is sick. Benita made each word a cement block.

"*¡Carajo! ¡No te creo!*" I don't believe you.

Charlotte sat up on the edge of her bed. She raked her hands through her hair, then threw it back, her chin towards the ceiling. The room was pitch-black. The rain had begun, rushing, pounding, spattering. It hit the window like handfuls of birdshot.

* * *

"It was a little clam" is what the fat man had said. He had rolled his eyes as he chewed. "They're always at the very bottom of the soda glass, waiting for me."

When he stood up, his stomach looked obscene, straining the buttons on his *guayabera*. He took Charlotte's briefcase. "Sit here," he said with a sloppy smile. His lips were a slash of red lipstick. "We're all bore-der 'n plywood, 'til the rain stops."

He said he was from Corpus Christi. He smelled of whiskey and of Joy de Patou, and his fingers were the rosy-beige of Vienna sausages. The gold ring on his pinky looked tight.

"Doesn't that pinch?" Charlotte ran her fingertip along his knuckle.

"Yes it do," he said, milking Charlotte's eyes. "Yes, it shore-ly do."

It was his good luck ring, he said. He'd put it on the day he graduated from Texas A&M. Now he had two hundred acres of coffee trees up in Xalapa, a fleet of rental trucks in Campeche, and a majority share in the Discoteque Chapultepec, behind the Capilla del Buen Viaje.

"You know the Capilla?" The man's eyes were small and blood-shot. "Block from Independencia? Place with the nigger Christ."

Charlotte suddenly realized that he was extremely drunk. "Course not," she said. "I just got here." She reached down under the table for her briefcase. There was a noxious smell.

"Mah ring don't bring me luck with the ladies." The man was staring at Charlotte's chest. He sniffed. "Both my wifes leff me. Yooo don't even want to sit with me."

Charlotte began to walk away, each step a moonwalk, or her shoes stuck in clumps of bog, the colored lights blinking on, then off, then on, like a disco, an old, old movie.

"Ooh, I a loney o dawg!" the man called, white and black, white! "I'm gonna snap this heah ring off with metal clippahs!" He was hollering. "Make mah fingah fattah 'en a zeppelin!"

∗ ∗ ∗

Silk on damask, and outside, the trees lashed against each other like angry lovers. A lull, and would it be Margarita Maza now, her face a tear-stained summer moon, tangling Charlotte's hair, catching, tearing out strands with her bracelet of rattling snail shells? Gooseflesh and bleach; nettles raining down on wet bark and riverbed stones. The power had blown out. Charlotte struck a match. The little flame, no larger than a fingernail, made the furniture quiver alive and dance, shadows warp around the walls. She lit a candle and set it on her dresser. She watched the flame flick straight up, shrink. She pulled open a drawer and plunged into stretch-lace and straps, hooks and hose and satin soft half-slips. A still leaden sky, and a wave's palms slid down the rim of sand, raking its fingers down, scooping out bras and panties and slips, then raining down, *teyolpat̢miqui,* fluffy piles on her bed. She would pull all her dresses off their hangers, suits and blouses, scoop-neck shirts and trousers, shoes and shoe trees and bottles of polish and lotion. She would take all the suitcases, jewelry, the trunks, perfumes, soaps, duffels and briefcases, shampoo in knotted plastic bags.

She set the candle on Max's dresser and pulled open the bottom drawer. In a sock: twenty *centenarios,* fifty peso coins. She drew out handfuls of *centenarios,* her wrists bending back and aching with the weight. And a small flocked velvet box: his malachite cuff links. A sharp-edged plastic box with his collar stays, a dirt-encrusted golf tee. Were there more *centenarios?* She pressed her palm down on each sock. She leaned in and felt in the very back of the drawer: a roughly cut square of silk. She brought it up to the light. It was stained, and crinkled dry with age. She rubbed it across the back of one hand. She thought of his moles, his hairy shoulders. She pushed the square of silk under the bed.

She reached down again into the far corner of the drawer, and her fingers wrapped around something small and hard, precisely the size of a thumb. It was a black shriveled thing, like a prune, or a date with a very long pit. She felt, at one end, a tiny beak.

"Benita," she whispered, and her throat shut tight. "*Me metiste al demonio.*" You sent me to the Devil.

She drove her fist into her own pillow. She left the hummingbird in the hollow.

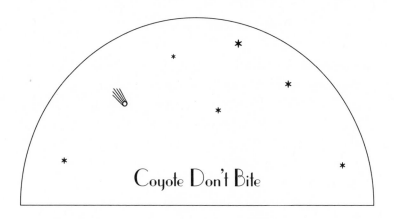

Coyote Don't Bite

The Deal

This is what I do: I buy pawn tickets outside the National Pawn Shop. Totally legit. Bunch of neckties, OK they put up this little sign. *Watch out for the coyotes,* it says. *Don't sell them your pawn tickets, 'cause they'll rip you off.* Course it's more elegant than that, hand-painted, yes indeed, and in a gold leaf frame. Hangs over the entrance.

I stand here on the sidewalk, 8:00 till 13:00 closing, Monday to Saturday. As if poor little Lupita López gets off the bus from Santa Noplace, some kind of dumbcluck. Shit! These old ladies got rhino hide. Fat and nasty, clutching their pawn tickets like the title to grand-pappy's cornfields.

Five minutes before closing time, this Lupita waddles up to me. She's squinting in the sun, smells of Tepito musk oil and Zest. Says she's got a ticket, gonna expire today, as in five minutes, for two chairs. Chairs. Pine, four legs each, no supports, red vinyl cushions. Pawnshop says they're worth 125, lent her 62.5, charged her 3%, and we're talkin' two months so it's 6%, that's 3.75, that's 36% annual, not too bad.

This is all thousands of pesos, you understand.

Deal is, I pay 62.5 plus 3.75, that's 66.25, I get the chairs, sell 'em for 125, that's net for me 58.7 less what I pay her.

She wants 57! So I get net 1.7 for hauling out two chairs? For bothering to unload 'em? For standing in this blazing glare, breathing this fume bomb of an excuse for an atmosphere? When my last deal was a ticket for one 12K pinky ring at 11:30?

Lady. Try like 5. Like 6. Like max max total max I am doing you a favor from the very bottom of my heart, and only because you are so bee-oo-tee-fool, 6.5.

She wants 25! And she's givin' me those squinty eyes, like a bird could land on her back, start pecking off the tsetse flies, and she'd just munch the grass.

I say 19. She says 22.

I say 19.5. She says 22.

I say 20. She says 22.

Lady, lady lady lady, look. Over there, those two big old wooden doors? The ones two stories tall covered with iron bumps? With the little gold framed sign there? They're closing them now! 19.

Twenty-two it is and I run, because when the pawnshop guards see me they start pushing the doors harder. But I'm saved by another Lupita, this one's skittling in behind me in old tennis shoes, face all screwed up like she's gonna cry, lacy slip hanging down below the housecoat, snotty little boy in hand. Course, they hold the door open for her.

I get in line, I give 'em my ticket, I pay the 66.25. And what do they give me? Two chairs. They're pine all right, four legs, no supports. Red vinyl cushions. But the legs are wobbly and the red vinyl cushions are slashed, like with a carpet cutter or something.

125, my doody. And they're heavy.

The Coyote

They say there was a coyote named Mochis. Mochis stood here on the sidewalk, just like me, day after day, year after year, rain, shine, whatever. Mochis had a wife and kid. And then another kid, and then another, and another, and things were getting tight. Mochis' wife worked in a dry cleaners, but then she got sick, some kind of female trouble. Mochis' mother broke her hip and had to move in, took the only good bed in the house, made Mochis and his wife sleep on the couch. Their roof collapsed in a rainstorm. Not long after, they got robbed, lost their color television. It was really bad.

Then one day, one real normal kind of day, you know, tickets on a couple of watches, a lady's silver and opal brooch, a clarinet, Mochis bought a pawn ticket on a chair. Just some ordinary kind of chair, mahogany with flowers carved on the back and a green velvet seat. Mochis paid it off, but when he tried to pick the chair up, he couldn't, it was so heavy. He asked 'em to hold it for him, and—cook me with the *pozole*—the neckties obliged.

Next day, Mochis was back with three of his boys. And with each one grabbing a leg, they heaved the chair up to their shoulders. They oomphed and groaned and they got it out the doors of the National Pawn Shop, and sweating and *ahhg*ing, they inched with it across the square. Then, their knees ready to buckle, they carried it down the steps to the subway. They rode the subway for an hour, but then they had to haul the chair out again, up the stairs, down ten city blocks, and then up four unpaved streets on a hillside, all rutted and pasty from the rains.

By the time Mochis and his boys got to their house they were holding that chair up like zombies. Mochis kicked the door open, the hell with Mama on the couch, with Gramma there on the bed: the four of them let it go. *D-CHOOK.* A leg broke off. And *centenarios,* fifty peso coins, started pouring out, all over the cement floor.

Well, I'll tell you what. Even me, Mr. A. Nobody (A. as in Absolutely), coyote at the National Pawn Shop, I know all about the lady who put her poodle in the microwave, to dry it off. And about the Kentucky Fried mouse, somehow got into the vat of batter. And that if you get a Pyramid Power chain letter and don't send in 10,000 pesos and pass copies on to eight friends asap, you'll be eaten alive by coyotes.

They say Mochis bought a ranch in Sinaloa. Set the wife up in her own dry-cleaning business. Got Gramma a new hip, bought a videocassette recorder and a Handycam. Took the boys to Disneyland.

My butt.

I can't figure what's with the slashes in the red vinyl cushions. 125, no way.

Scenario 1, Lupita brought 'em in like this. See, they lend you 50% of the value, so maybe Lupita did a routine on Necktie. You know, If I can't pay for my baby daughter's operation, she'll be crippled for life. If I can't pay the lawyer, I'll be thrown out onto the street, tiny fatherless children and furniture and dogs and turkeys and bunnies. The police took my husband's ice cream cart and if I can't get him another one, and and and.

Scenario 2, Necktie gets one look at Yours Truly, a familiar face indeed, takes my hard-earned money, goes in back to the storeroom, slashes the cushions, and brings 'em out.

Could be 1, could be 2. But I got nothin' doin' all afternoon, and it don't say nothin' 'bout the red vinyl cushions on the ticket. I decide to take this to the Complaints Department.

The Complaints Department

They make the ceilings low in places like this on purpose. Neckties 'specially rude. Benches extra hard. My advantage is, here they don't know me that good. Here they think I'm a regular customer. I take my ticket, No. 7, yes, my lucky number. I put my two chairs down, sit on the bench, set my legs up on the red vinyl cushions. It's only 13:10 P.M.

At 13:30 I notice there's no windows in here.

14:45 I begin counting the little bits of cushion foam that have fallen on the floor. 23. Oops, 24. I pick a few more bits off, flick 'em across the floor.

15:20 I look at the Lupita sitting across from me and say, "What's your complaint?" She does a yellow-eyed squinty squinty. She tosses a gold watch from one palm to the other and back again. And again. It makes a heavy slapping noise. Then her boyfriend, 150 kilos of pimples packed into a Houston Oilers T-shirt, says, "Shut Up."

Oh, well, I was planning on doing that anyway.

While later Lupita nods off. Her head goes back against the wall and her mouth opens, just a little. She's breathing deep, her neck out, the color of molasses, her arms crossed over her chest, rising, falling. Boyfriend pulls something out from his back pocket. It looks like a comic book, but he keeps it in his lap, his hands on it like two big hams. Lupita begins to snore, just a little, *click* breathe, *click* breathe. Boyfriend gives her a long sideways look. Then he picks up the comic book, holds it in front of his face.

Everyone can see what it is: BEAUTIFUL NURSES GET HOT.

The old lady next to me starts crossing her legs one way, then crossing her legs the other way. She beetles her brows and starts coughing. She's got nothin' to cough, it's a dry *hack hack*.

Lupita snorts awake. She gets one look at BEAUTIFUL NURSES and she socks Boyfriend in the eye with the watch.

"You bitch!" he says. He grabs his eye as if he could clench it, or hold it in. Then he starts to moan, a low noise, like a wounded dog.

"I fuckin' told you, you animal!" she screams. Her voice is like needles in my ear, the room's so small. She grabs BEAUTIFUL NURSES off his lap and starts tearing off the corners, ripping out the center. "You pig!" she rips. "You horny donkey!" She's stamping her feet, little bits of comic book are flying like chicken feathers. "You, you," ahhh, she says it: "COYOTE."

It's 17:16 P.M. Boyfriend's been long gone. No. 3 was called forty-five minutes ago. No. 4 went fast. While No. 5 was up, more people came into our little room. The shreds of BEAUTIFUL NURSES have mingled with my foam bits on the floor. There, in the shadows under her bench.

Slap, slap. Back and forth.

Lupita has a body like a tamale, round and compact, firm but maybe easy to bite into. She's No. 6, and there she goes.

The Director

Is it true that loving fat women is the same as loving skinny women? It seems to me that if they're fat, there's more of them. Rich guys, they like skinny women.

I remember when the Director of the National Pawn Shop started driving up to work in a black Lincoln Continental. And then he started getting driven up in the Lincoln Continental. And then he started getting driven up in the Lincoln Continental with his assistant and, man, was she one skinny broad. She looked like she was made of toothpicks, all angles and knees and elbows and a long long neck. But you could tell: this was an Expensive Babe. She had a good haircut, had it fixed so the roots didn't show, and lots of gold jewelry, nice stuff, not like what you see at the National Pawn Shop. He'd come around to the other side of the car and open the door for her, and she'd stick out one leg, Betty Boop up to Yin-Yang, flash her thirty trillion peso smile. He'd have to pull her out, them leather seats were so very low 'n cushy. Then they'd prance by us coyotes, in through the main entrance, Miss Chin-In-The-Air, Mr. Double-Breasted Blazer.

"Morning," he'd mutter under his breath, to the line of Lupitas, us coyotes with our hands jammed in our pockets. To no one in particular.

But the assistant started getting fat. At first you'd hardly notice, 'cept that she wore tight miniskirts and you could see the panty line. Every day it got a little more noticeable until, I swear, her ass looked like a pat of butter with two knife marks on it. She got a double chin, her cheeks swelled up, her knees blobby, and before you knew it, it was in all the newspapers: Director of the National Pawn Shop thrown in the tank for embezzlement.

What a bad wave.

The Decision

What's 125? What can that buy? Tacos for ten at the corner. With Coca-Colas. Or a taxi for the day. About eight liters of guanabana sherbet. Lupita's done now, and I'm No. 7.

We all have to make choices in life: four liters of guanabana (that's 8 less I figure 4) down the pipes. I grab my chairs and run.

"Miss!" She sure walks fast. "Miss!" She's out the double doors and I'm still a couple of meters behind her, the backs of the chairs slamming my shoulders, the legs rubbing my thighs, they're going to be all red and maybe bleeding.

I'm gettin' hoarse. "Miss!"

There at the far side of the square, by the subway, she stops. The sky is a weepy gray bowl, and the National Palace, the Cathedral, they all look yellow brown, like in old photographs. A flock of pigeons sweeps up, and the fluttering and cooing weaves into the cars and buses and taxis going around the square, the Mexican flag in the center, gigantic, snapping *snic . . . snac.*

Her knuckles are jammed into her waist, her feet planted like trunks.

(Is this a great country?)

"Hey!" she shouts. Raindrops begin to dot the ground, and I feel a warm splash on my forehead. A bus changes gears and screeches to a halt. I'm hobbling up closer, but I still can't hear what she's saying. I let the raindrop roll down my nose, and I catch it with the tip of my tongue.

Then I hear her.

"Hey!" she says. "What makes you think I want your fuckin' chairs?"

The Doctor

"What makes you think I'd want you?" That's what Ramón the cripple, who is actually Dr. Ramón Limón, said on *Savage Tears.*

Then we got a shot of Casilda's face, her jaw dropped open, her perfect painted nails (diamond on every finger) fluttering up to her cheeks.

To be continued next Tuesday.

Dr. Limón sure fooled her. Once the grandfather died, everybody knew Dr. Ramón Limón was going to inherit everything—millions and billions and zillions of pesos. Investments in New York and Acapulco and Japan, racehorses, restaurants, nightclubs. But nobody had seen Dr. Limón since he was a child. His parents both died of yellow fever when they were on a safari in the Amazon, and so little Ramón was raised by Indians. Then he became a heart surgeon at a world famous hospital in Río de Janeiro, Brazil. He came back to Mexico City to hear the reading of the will, get his money, and find himself a Mexican wife to take back to Brazil.

The trick was, Dr. Limón had to find a girl who loved him for himself, not for all his money. So he disguised himself as Ramón, a distant cousin from Torreón, childhood friend and agent for Dr. Limón (who was, but of course, very busy doing heart surgery in Brazil). And Ramón, the distant cousin from Torreón, was not only poor, he was also a cripple, stuck in a rickety wheelchair.

Casilda is Dr. Limón's third cousin, and the girl all the aunts want him to marry. She's tall, she's thin, she's blonde, and it's practically arranged. The problem is, Dr. Limón won't come up from Brazil. And this cousin the cripple is getting in the way, asking them to put in an elevator so he can get upstairs—the nerve!—blocking the hallway, leaving muddy wheel marks on the imported tropical wood floors. Just being ugly and crippled, you know.

When no one's looking, Ramón reaches under his ratty little blanket and whips out his cellular phone. He calls his stockbroker in New York, or the race track to see how his horses are doing.

Rosa, the daughter of the maid, takes care of Ramón. She's round and bubbly, a sweet soul. She fixes the wobbly wheel on his chair, she knits him a new blanket. She's studying to be a nurse, and late at night, after she's brought Ramón a glass of warm milk, she tells him her dreams.

Well, one thing leads to another and Ramón, overcome with love and respect for Rosa, reveals himself. And Rosa will be Mrs. Dr. Ramón Limón, wife of the head heart surgeon at the world famous hospital in Brazil, owner of all that stuff!

The End

And Lupita's curling her lip like she's gonna pound me one if I don't put my tail between my legs and creep away.

"Oh come on, baby." I give 'er my coyote smile. "Coyote don't bite."

Suddenly the sky cracks. The rain is coming down in a solid silver sheet. I hold one of the chairs out to her. She grunts, but she takes the chair and we both, both at the same time, flip 'em over our heads and start running across the square, scrambling toward the subway.

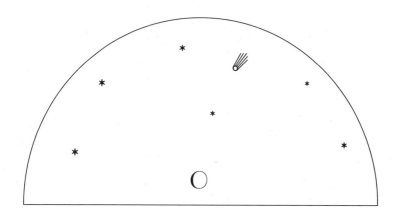

The Maya live in white plastered huts, thatch-roofed, dark little boxes. A cross between County Rye and the Kalahari, he thinks, speeding down the narrow two-lane highway. His rented black sedan arrows through a village, then open country, low scrub. Another village, he downshifts. Children sit on a stoop, dogs pant in the clay-colored dust. Squat women in white sack dresses eye the car warily. Flashes of red, rose, jungle green. A bare-chested man butchers a pig. Its squealing fades like the rattle in the car's air-conditioning. Past a knot of palms: a cathedral, vaulted chambers stretching, Ecce Homo, towards the very center of the dome of the afternoon sky.

He is Albert Andrade. This is Neptune, with televisions. There: he can see a green cathode flickering. There, whiz by, bicycle, roadside papaya stand, under the hammock—in there!—chickens scratching, open country, low scrub. Eiko holds out her hand, saffron, thin-fingered. A claw, Albert senses in the corner of his mind, speckled with black and yellow capsules. "Just take one," she says. "You'll want two." She has a laugh like a piccolo. "Later you'll need three." He takes four, a swig of Diet Coke, shifts into fifth. Low scrub, open country.

* * *

They met in Florence, at a table under a loden-green awning, next to the Uffizi. It was June, the swallows flit and lit like cinders silly in a breeze.

"I prefer Moschino," she said. She only drank kir, champagne with a bloodlet of kirsch, down in one gulp, her cheeks and chin flushed gold, her eyes crossed. "Oh!" she'd say. "Oh!" The bubbles burned her nose. People passed by, Americans in lollipop golf shirts, Germans, French too thin or too fat, Australians, an African in a tie-dyed dashiki, his face darker than the center purple of a bruise. Eiko rolled her eyes and jitter-mumbled, "Punch perm." At him? At the African? He pinched her thigh; she was wearing a rubber skirt. A twilight whiff from across an ocean, a frisson: he reached across the table and raked his hands through her hair. It fell over her shoulders in strands, black corn silk, silk on silk. They ordered two more kirs. Then two more and the sun came down, blinding the sky. The spires turned black, swallows and pigeons went to roost, and the street lamps throbbed, luxurious electric.

Albert said, "What is Moschino?"

∗ ∗ ∗

These are the things that Albert knows about Eiko: that she loves Hieronymus Bosch and she is bored with Michelangelo. Her purse is stuffed with packets of Chung Chan soy sauce, she nibbles sugared ginger in the mornings, sometimes with acid, sometimes with the tiniest shard of *shabu* which she smokes with a delicate, sucking noise. And she always drinks tea, not coffee. Never coffee (that smells like medicine). She has a two-week supply of yellow jackets. And she likes to make little kisses around the crown of his head.

This too: that her father plays golf in the Genting Highlands, that she spent summers at a tennis camp in San Diego. That she met there a Mexican girl, Ifigenia, who invited her to Guadalajara, who showed her a steel vault crammed with oxygen tanks, boxes of dried eggs and vacuum-packed tomato soup, a wall of rifles and automatics, a drawerful of Swiss pistols.

Such large things, bigger than she is. Eiko, Albert thinks, Eiko, little Eiko, flat-chested child. Amazing this, amazing that, her words clunking along like tiny feet shuffling in Big Sister's shoes. Little kisses around the crown of his head, around the hairline. Behind his ears, along the rim of his collarbone.

Albert said, "Where are the Genting Highlands?"

* * *

Eiko's wrists smell of Chanel No. 5, a musky sweet expensive smell, and her hair of something light, jasmine in the shade. Genting Highlands, Albert thinks. Gentle High Land. Ting Land. He thinks he hears a tinkling of distant bells.

Albert remembers now that he once met a Malaysian, his second-year studying art history. His name was John, and somehow they were talking, beers in hand, Lucky Strikes fuming from their stained fingers. The room had a tattered poster of Che, posed like a rock star, a dirty linoleum floor, a curly-haired girl's marmalade cat. John said, "Imperialism," such an age-nineteen word, "you don't know imperialism." John laughed a big beer laugh, his teeth mint Chiclets. "They look so civilized now, in their white floppy golf hats, all ha-ha-ha up in the Genting Highlands. When the Japanese invaded, they took any truck, any jeepney, any bicycle they could lay their hands on. My grandfather was riding his bicycle home from the laboratory. A soldier took it and shoved him into a ditch."

And then they threw the British out of Singapore.

Albert imagines the grandfather in a batik skirt and plastic flip-flops, rolling over and over rocks and the stubs of cut bushes.

* * *

Florence was one week ago, now Eiko says, "Stop," and bangs the window with her fist. "I want to see that pyramid."

"O," in his mind Albert hears "O." He reminds himself he is Albert-O, Great-grandfather lost the ranch in Hermosill-O and came to California, the O's caught on the barbed wire between two cultures. The barrel of Ifigenia's Swiss pistol, Edvard Munch's "The Scream," which museum is that in? Spagetti-O's.

"O-kay," he says and he pulls over. Eiko darts out with her camera. He stays in the car, beads of sweat on his forehead. He feels cold blood moving around the capillaries in his temples, circling his sternum, under the skin of his calves. The air-conditioning squeals. He is a glass of iced Diet Coke, his mind freezing but liquid, the bubbles of gas, ooooo's, all gone, flat. Oolong tea.

Eiko does not ask questions. But Albert wants her to, he now realizes. He wants her to ask, When did they build these pyramids? Why is Uxmal different from Chichén, from Labná, Sayil, Dzibilchaltún? Who is Chac? What is Puuc? Tell me about the books. You know (she might tap her nails across his chest), the books.

Must have been the mushrooms, that was Oaxaca, where did they stay? The Marqués Del Valle? Or the Presidente? Albert is oozing Diet Coke from behind his ears. He feels bitter rivulets, lighter than water, down his neck, in his armpits. Eiko has run up the broken steps to the top of the pyramid. It is more a pile of gray rubble, short grasses covering its sides like a lush green fur. There are flashes of orange and blue, but the few dark bushes and a tree have been hacked down with a machete. A coralillo spills over one side, and the ground below is littered with bright pink petals.

"Albert!" she shouts, her voice too high, like an unhappy bird. "Albert-O!" She is swinging her hips, waving her arms. "Albert! Run up here with me!" She swings, she jiggles.

Drugs, Albert thinks. "*Solo di' non!*" Just say no! Eiko said. They had looked at each other like startled rabbits. Then they laughed, and pounded the metal-top bar table with their fists, and tried to keep drinking their Coronas, but they kept giggling and got bubbles up their noses.

Albert rolls down the window. "No." He wipes his forehead with his palm, Diet Coke on Diet Coke. "I don't want to climb any pyramid. I feel like Diet Coke."

"What?" Eiko starts hopping.

"*Allegrissimo. Appassionato. A prima vista.*"

"What?"

Albert moves on to "B" words: "*Bagliore. Barzelletta. Bracciole.*"

The sun is behind the pyramid. A five o'clock moon, parchment thin, peers into his windshield.

"What?"

Albert leans over and puts his hand into her purse. He moves his fingers over her Gold Pfeil wallet, bulging, buttery leather. Her lipsticks, small and cold. Her passport, her brush, her box of Kleenex, her vial of Chanel No. 5. Her broken bikini top, her *Brown's Guide to Shopping Paris.* The packets of Chung Chan soy sauce slide along the bottom. The bottles. He empties out two yellow jackets, swallows them with his saliva, Diet Coke.

"Limburger!" Eiko aims her camera down at the car.

A small boy sits on the curb across the street, scowling. He is wearing a torn gray T-shirt that says "Six Flags Over Georgia." He wanted a tip to watch the car. But Albert does not get out. He runs his hands along the warm plastic of the steering wheel. Slowly, then faster, with a rhythm.

This is the pyramid where a Spanish priest burned the Maya's books. All but three. One is in a museum in Dresden. Albert has seen it, lying in its dark glass case, bound in a flaking jaguar skin. The other is in Paris, or Madrid. Albert tries, but he cannot remember what is in them. He thinks about the third book. It was found only ten years ago, in a cave somewhere on a cattle ranch in Chiapas. The specialists at the University of Texas at Austin and the Universidad Nacional spent three years restoring, deciphering, divining, interpreting. Then, with great fanfare—a press conference, a cocktail party (later, a series of lectures)—they announced that the book described, with perfect accuracy, the orbit of Venus.

* * *

Eiko has fallen over, and she is tumbling down the rubble of the steps, over the soft grasses. Albert grips the steering wheel and bites his lip. Her small body lies at the bottom, inert. But, ah, up she jumps, hip hop and jiggle. She's got a jagged orange flower in her hand. A bird of paradise.

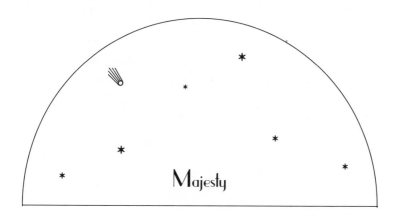

Majesty

"It is a long tail certainly," said Alice . . .
"but why do you call it sad?"

Ana Guadalupe María Teresa García Ponçet y Rivera's feet, shod in the smallest size of purple plastic thongs from the gift and tobacco shop, almost touch the floor. She tugs at the strap of her black maillot as she studies the breakfast menu, a square of calf's hide strewn with hand-colored etchings of jojoba and saguaro.

"I will have a triple banana split with extra cherries," she tells the waitress.

The waitress is a strawberry blonde with an upturned nose. She smells slightly of coconut. She begins to scribble down the order, but stops, one arm akimbo, and winks. "Your mother's gonna go for this?"

"My mother is meeting me at the swimming pool," Ana says, and stares the girl full in the face. "I would like," she draws the words out now like saltwater taffy, "a triple banana split with extra cherries."

The waitress scribbles this down.

"And," Ana continues, tucking one ankle under her bottom, "a double espresso."

"Room number?" The waitress's voice is stony.

Ana claps the room key on the marble table top. "One twenty-three," she says. "García Ponçet y Rivera."

"What? García?"

"García. One twenty—"

"Yeah, okay." The waitress bares her teeth.

* * *

The swimming pool is cast in shadows until midmorning. The room is a shambles before it's been made up. And there are no cartoons on, only shows where a man with a microphone stalks the aisles of spectators, who stand up and shout things in spurts, who wear strange clothing, pants with elastic waistbands.

Up and down the thickly carpeted sand-colored corridors Ana skips and shuffles, listening for voices, of children complaining, old men, the television. *"Pero ya compraste seis del mismito color, oye," "Watashi no huto momo o monde kudasai—"* "Do we *have* to see the Grand Canyon?" "It was *your* idea!" a man yells at who knows? None of this is the least bit interesting.

On the second floor the ice machine groans, caterwauls, spits cubes into a bin. Ana takes one and draws it along the wallpaper, the closed doors, with one hand, then the other, until it melts to a nub at the end of the corridor.

On the third floor she finds one of the maids' carts, stocked with boxes of purple Kleenex, rolls of three-ply purple toilet paper, sewing kits disguised as matchbooks, jojoba shampoo, a vase crammed with cut orchids. She stands on tiptoe and snatches a handful of foil-wrapped Good Night chocolates.

"Buenos días," she calls out to the maid.

The maid, startled, nearly jumps out of the bathroom, her hands in too-big rubber gloves.

"*Ah, Señorita Ani,*" she says, and her soft brown face breaks with a smile. "*Buenos días.*"

* * *

There is grass, lots of grass. Little houses with lush patios ring the grass, and old men in lollipop-colored shirts drive purple covered carts along a winding asphalt path. Ana walks the perimeter, on the lookout for Johnny the bloodhound puppy. She has found him twice now, sitting on the asphalt path just outside his patio, taking the sun. She has never seen his person, only read his dog tag:

MY NAME IS JOHNNY

GENEROUS REWARD

334-0987

"Toot! Toot!" an old man shouts at her from his little cart. She skitters to the side and he whizzes by her, tipping his visor, laughing.

She walks along the path past the duck pond, past a series of amoeba-shaped sand traps, and comes to the patio of Johnny's house. Through the iron bars she can see a white-haired lady squatting down to tend a row of pansies.

"Where's Johnny?" Ana calls to her.

The lady twists her chin around, and then, slowly, as if in great pain, she stands up. She is wearing plaid shorts and an old button-down collar shirt. Her tennis shoes are caked with mud.

"How do you know my Johnny?" she says, approaching the fence. She is very tan, and her skin looks leathery.

"I saw him yesterday," Ana says. "He is nice."

"Yes, well." The woman knocks her trowel against an iron bar, to shake off a dirt clod. "He's having his milk in the kitchen."

"Oh," Ana says. She scrunches her face and scratches the back of one knee with the toe of her thong.

"Where's your mother, dear?" The old lady is squinting.

* * *

There are palm trees, lots of palm trees, and a lumpy brown mountain that looks like a camel's back. It is February, a time to be in school. The lobby bar is serving complimentary mugs of chicken bouillon; *nuevo flamenco* bleats from discreetly placed stereo speakers. Ana is perched on a barstool, slurping a cherry-flavored sparkling water with a straw. At one of the tables, a woman in a houndstooth check blazer and a mango Hermès scarf sits curled over her crossword puzzle. A Japanese man works his way towards the glass doors, slowly, using a walker. He hunches his wishbone shoulders as he lets his weight sink with each careful step. Ana pats her thongs against her heels to the clack of castanets; she shreds her purple cocktail napkin into strips thin as pencils, rolled thin as yarn, threads of cotton, fiber-optic hairs maybe.

"*Pues hay todo tipo de escuelas,*" Well there are all kinds of schools, someone says in a high voice behind her ear. Ana jerks around, and a man, or a boy—or a woman (for an instant she is not sure)— slides onto the barstool next to hers. His face is the color of molasses, delicate, smooth, but he is too tall, she decides, to be a boy.

"*¿Sabes?*" Do you know, he goes on in a languid, sleepy voice, "there are schools that will teach you to make hats? Or to cut hair? To write sonnets and songs, how to play chess?" He is from Guadalajara, she can tell. His alligator watchband is loose around his hairless wrist. He is wearing a white T-shirt and baggy shorts. He is drinking something that looks like apple soda. "How to trade futures and options even." He has a thick gold rope of a necklace that he pulls out and twists around his thumb.

"What are futures and options?" Ana ventures to ask.

The man opens his eyes wide as walnut shells. He brushes a strand of lank brown hair behind his ear. "Certainties and maybes," he says. They both consider this for a moment. A woman with a tightly pulled chignon leans down to peck the cheek of the woman in the houndstooth blazer. The Japanese man has made it out the door. *"Ike no ishi wa shinwa no tori!"* he says (she thinks), raising one fist towards the swimming pool. *"No yoni yuga de furyu desu."* The guitars strum softly, madly.

The man puts his elbows on the bar and begins to puff a cheroot, trying to get it lit. The smoke has a cloying smell, like fresh-cut grass. This reminds Ana of her uncles' cigars, Davidoffs they keep in tropical wood boxes in their dining rooms, and clip with metal clippers. She slurps the last of her sparkling water with a noise that sounds like a ribbon of paper caught in an electric fan.

The woman with the chignon is batting her arms now, as if to get out from under a sheet, furiously.

"Sorry, Alex!" the bartender calls over his shoulder. He is polishing a tumbler with a small purple towel. "This is a no smoking bar. You could—"

"Oh," he says, as if charmed, "that's all right." His English is crisp as a toasted biscuit. "It tastes better from a hookah anyway." In one fluid motion he plunges the cheroot into the amber snifter and glides out the glass doors, past the Japanese man (now leaning over the front of his walker, his face tilted stiffly to the sun), past the clay pots of saguaro and aloe, past the croquet lawn still submerged in the shade of the hotel, towards the swimming pool.

From her barstool Ana can see his small figure leap . . . and disappear beneath the shimmering lapis lazuli.

* * *

Puddles of pool water flash on the tiles. A waiter scoots by with a tray of bright orange drinks. Alex is lying on a plastic strap chaise longue, leafing through an oversized full-color magazine. He is still wearing his T-shirt, plucking at his chest to help it dry in the sun. His hair is slicked back, and parted down the center. Ana sits cross-legged on the next chaise, slurping a virgin banana daiquiri with a straw. The breeze has raised goose bumps on her legs and arms, and her eyes sting.

Alex says, "I think it's just fabulous that Princess Stephanie had a baby with her bodyguard." He is talking to a much older man who has the bulging eyes of a troll. The old man is slathering lotion on his arms. His flesh hangs in gray, leathery folds. His white hair is thick as a paintbrush and points up straight over his massive forehead.

"I mean, look at his face," Alex says. "Those sloe-eyed smirks."

"He has the face of a turnip," the old man says. He is wearing a zebra stripe bikini. His toes are startlingly long. He may be an American.

"Look!" Alex holds up the open magazine. "Stephanie's put sunglasses on the baby!" Ana recognizes last week's *Hola*. "She's pushing the pram!"

"Hmm," the old man says. He tucks the bottle of lotion under his *Wall Street Journal* and stretches out on the chaise, his back to the sun.

"Hmmmmm," he says again, and closes his eyes.

Ana sucks on her straw, then blocks it with the tip of her tongue. She pulls the straw out, holds it up, one finger on the other end. Banana slush defies gravity.

"*Mi mamá siempre lee* Hola," My mother always reads *Hola*, Ana says. She blinks, hard.

"Hmm," Alex says. He waves at a blonde woman in a parrot-green sarong, who waves back from the other side of the pool, near the clay pots of saguaro, the cabañas. "Alex!" she calls, and blows a kiss.

An airplane passes overhead, then into a tuft of cloud above the camel's-back mountain. The cloud seems bleached, tenuous.

"I like the pictures of Princess Di," Ana says.

The old man has begun to snore, a gentle *click-click,* like muffled castanets. Alex continues leafing through the magazine. He holds it sideways for a better look at something.

* * *

A lunch buffet is set up near the cabañas. Ana wraps herself in a sheet-sized purple towel and takes a plate.

"*Buenas tardes,*" Good afternoon, the chef says to her. He is from somewhere near the border, she can tell. He is wearing an enormous chef's hat and a starched tunic.

"*Buenas,*" Ana says and piles her plate with chocolate pudding.

"Wouldn't you like some lobster salad?" The chef seems concerned. He is waving an unusually long jagged knife. He is standing next to an ice sculpture of a camel. "A slice of roast beef with a little juice?"

"No." Ana is trying to slide a wedge of vanilla cake onto the serving spatula, but it keeps slipping back onto the platter.

The chef purses his lips and grins. "What will your mother say when she sees your plate?"

"I can have whatever I want," Ana says, still struggling with the cake. The chef doesn't seem to have an answer for that. She grabs the wedge of cake with her hand. It lands on the pudding with a *plop.*

"*Atsui. Yogan mitai,*" a Japanese woman with a pinched face whispers to herself, apparently. She is wearing a grape-colored Gucci sheath and matching platform sandals. The chef serves her a slab of roast beef and dollop of horseradish sauce, and she minces towards the salads, the jumbles of bell peppers and baby corn, pine nuts and cherry tomatoes.

* * *

There is a spa, a very big spa. It has a juice bar where one can snack on chilled carrot sticks and order cocktails: cucumber lemon and carrot; cucumber beet and carrot; papaya; blueberry strawberry squeeze of mandarin orange.

"Cucumber blueberry," Ana says. She is barefoot. She is wearing her black maillot.

"*Fuchi,*" Yuck. Alex crinkles his nose. His face is scrubbed fresh, the skin smooth as an olive. He is wrapped in a snow white terrycloth robe; he is wearing purple plastic thongs from the gift and tobacco shop. He is leafing through a large glossy magazine. He smells slightly of Chanel No. 5, or is it Ivoire? Something her mother would wear.

"You smell," Ana says, and bites a carrot stick. The man behind the counter switches on the blender. As it whirrs to a stop, Alex is saying "*you,*" with a sneer, jabbing the edge of his magazine at her chest. "And why do *you* follow me around?"

"I'm not following you around," Ana says. "I can sit at the juice bar anytime I like." She slaps her room key on the marble countertop. "I can order anything I like."

"You can't have tequila, or cigarettes," Alex says, staring at the man behind the bar. The man has fully defined biceps. He is wearing a purple T-shirt with the name of the hotel emblazoned across the chest in Times Roman Italic.

"Papaya celery!" Alex calls out.

"Okeydokey," the man says, and switches on a second blender.

Ana waits for the machine to stop. "I can so," she says. Her eyes glitter with outrage. "I can so have tequila and cigarettes and I've had them every night this week." She rests one elbow on the counter and gazes at the man.

"Stop staring, you little nitwit," Alex says, and pulls the collar of his terrycloth robe across his throat. From a stereo speaker near the ceiling, a sitar hums and an old woman's feathery voice begins to chant strange words.

"¡Alex! ¡Te encontré!" I found you! It's a short plump girl who may be Venezuelan, or perhaps Colombian. She's doing the cha-cha now, giggling. "Let's go again tonight!" She's halfway through the door to the locker room.

"Ten-thirty?"

The girl seems to be all teeth. Her hair is an unnatural yellow.

"Ten-forty-five, ciao!"

Ana snatches his magazine. "¡Oye!" Hey! Alex sniffs. He rolls his eyes, crosses his arms across his chest. She moistens her finger with her tongue and turns the page. There is a photograph of a blonde woman, her hipbones jutting out, wearing Ana's same maillot. *Points of interest: a strappy back, a scoop neck.* Ana takes a sip of the cucumber blueberry cocktail. It needs sugar, desperately. *Calvin Klein swimwear,* the small print says. *$163 at Neiman Marcus.*

Alex has moved to the far end of the juice bar and is hunched over a disarranged *Wall Street Journal.* He makes loud rustling noises, going through the paper too quickly. The feathery voice is lower now, the music sweeter, slightly faster, like spindles of afternoon rain.

Gracefully placed details add a soupçon of interest, Ana reads. She sucks in her cheeks, she fans her fingers. But her cheeks are plump with baby fat; her fingernails sadly blunt. She chews her lip. *Have a Hat Attack.* Ana turns the page, and an eye the size of her hand stares back at her, the pupil reflecting a tiger lily. She is about to ask for some sugar when a red-haired man with a mustache pokes his head in the doorway.

"Ms. García Ponçet y Rivera?" he calls out, beaming at Alex. He is wearing a purple T-shirt. His hair is kinky. He looks about forty, but it is hard to tell.

"It's for me," Ana says, tossing down the magazine.

"You!" The red-haired man has a California accent. His laugh sounds like macaroni noodles shaken in a box. He holds open the door to the massage rooms.

"Ciao," Alex says, and gives a *thwat* to the newspaper.

* * *

"Is this your first time?" The red-haired man is washing his hands at a small sink in the corner. The voice with the sitar is higher and nasal now, chanting something like *"Oo wah no, oo wah na no."*

"Nooooooo," Ana says. The lights have been dimmed, and she is sitting with her legs dangling off the side of the massage table. She tugs at the strap of her maillot.

"How do you want to feel today?" he asks.

"Oh, I don't know," Ana says, and lies down on her stomach.

"No, no, no," the man laughs. "First you need to take that bathing suit off. I'll step out for a minute and you lie down on your stomach. You can cover yourself with this." He pulls at the edge of a sheet that has been tucked around the table.

When the man comes back in the room, he announces: "We will do lavender and cucumber."

Ana puts her chin on the backs of her hands. "My mother always has yling ylang and vanilla."

"Oh my God!" the man says. He giggles. "You're much too young for that." He splashes something onto his palm. "Let's do lavender and cucumber. *Trust me.*" He begins to run a fragrant oil across her shoulder blades, then kneads it into the narrow ropes of muscle along her spine. "Cucumber oil is for sunburn, and freckles," the man says quietly. "You look like you're spending a lot of time in the swimming pool."

"Hmmm," Ana says, and squeezes her eyes shut. She feels the oil run across the small of her back, her elbows, wrists, the nape of her neck, like a Cuernavaca morning, like a sitar, something in the shadow.

"You're going to get an extra massage, you're so tiny!" the man chuckles, working her calves now. But Ana doesn't hear anything else he says, because she falls fast asleep, until another sharp and sweeter scent wakes her.

"Lavender," the red-haired man is saying, "is for headaches, for anxiety." And he makes tiny circles with his fingertips behind her ears.

* * *

There is steam, really, a lot of steam. It hits Ana in the face like a punch. "Ahg!" she says. She collapses on the tile bench. In a moment she recovers and tries to make out the other figure through the mist.

"Hi," she says.

"*Buenas,*" Alex says.

"Ha! So you're a girl!"

"I was in the men's steam room yesterday," he says. "So don't draw any conclusions."

"Ha!" Ana says again, weakly.

They sit silently for a while, their limbs limp in the heat.

"Where's your mother?" he says at last. He sounds provoked.

"I'm meeting her by the swimming pool." Ana smooths her towel and stretches out on her back. She adds, "My mother lets me do whatever I want," but senses that this is unnecessary.

"Well . . ." Alex says very slowly. His voice trails off in the heavy air.

A set of nozzles near the ceiling begins to blast in fresh steam. The noise is deafening, then stops with a sudden hiss. A stubby-legged woman in a dolphin-colored bikini comes in and sits with them for a few minutes. She keeps sweeping her hair off her neck and twisting it into a knot, and sighing. Then she leaves.

Alex wraps himself in a towel and shoves open the heavy glass door. As the steam rushes out, Ana can see his face suddenly tense. "Come on out of here," he says. "You shouldn't be in here alone." He reaches down and pulls her up by the arm. "Come on."

* * *

A clutch of violinists, a cellist, and a flautist are playing Mozart. Flower arrangements the size of peacocks' tails dot the lobby, in the corners, on pink marble pedestals. An especially large arrangement of parrot tulips, thistle, and red-speckled orchids sits on the mantel, where a gas fire flicks soundlessly in the grate. Ana is wearing her maillot, her purple plastic thongs, and a sheet-sized towel like a poncho.

"No room!" Alex cries from his purple loveseat when he sees her shuffling through the lobby. "No room!"

"There's tons of room," Ana says, eyeing the tufted purple armchair pulled up to one side of the coffee table.

A waiter swishes by with a dish of lemon slices.

"Have a toad's brain," Alex says, and waves an open palm over the low table. There is a silver teapot, two cups on saucers, cream and sugar, a plate of paper-thin finger sandwiches, and a silver bowl of candied chestnuts.

"Those are *marrons glacées*," Ana says and she sticks her tongue out. She climbs into the chair and tucks one ankle under her bottom.

"Have an apple chutney sandwich."

Ana pops a candied chestnut into her mouth. "No thanks," she says, working the sugary mash with her jaws.

Alex is wearing a white double-breasted linen jacket and trousers. A cellophane-wrapped cigar peeks out from his front pocket. He looks as if he would like to reach across the coffee table and slap her, but he says, "Why is Neiman Marcus like a jar of anchovy paste?"

Ana screws up her face, trying to think. She pours herself a cup of tea and stirs in eleven and one-half spoonfuls of sugar. She stares at Alex's shoes, black and cream spectators, exactly like her mother's.

"I don't know," she finally admits. "What?"

"I haven't the slightest idea," he says and he looks at his watch.

"Alex!" It's a woman with platinum hair teased into a poof on top of her head. She's carrying shopping bags in both hands, struggling towards the elevators.

"Ciao!" Alex blows her a kiss as she disappears behind the concierge's desk. "Have a look at this," he says to Ana. He leans over the arm of the loveseat and slips her a glossy magazine with a photograph of Queen Elizabeth in a tam-o'-shanter shaped hat. MAJESTY, it says, in skinny yellow letters.

Ana winces and hands back the magazine. She says, "The Queen has the face of a turnip." She rubs her ear with her towel.

"The Queen must be related to Princess Stephanie's bodyguard, then." Alex balances his saucer on his knee, holding the cup with his pinky out. "Olduvai Gorge," he muses. "Perhaps."

"Princess Di is very nice." Ana rolls her eyes and sinks into the chair. She slips off her thongs and curls her toes around the rim of the coffee table.

"Everything all right for you this afternoon?" A waitress in a black uniform and a white pinafore sets down a pitcher of hot water. There is a surge of violins, a silver trill of flute. "Princess Di is very—" Alex twists his gold chain around his thumb. He pats the cushion of the loveseat. "Come here, I'll show you something," he says. He spreads MAJESTY across their laps. "Look," he commands. "Princess Michael of Kent." He taps a fingernail on the page. "She's wearing that stunning hibiscus raincoat, on her way out of Annabel's. Look, look! at this Serena Stanhope, she's better than a soap opera star! See, she's going to marry Viscount Linley." He leafs through the pages now, quickly. Peachy-skinned women in enormous hats snip ribbons with monstrous scissors, kiss bloated bald children. The Duchess of York leans over the hospital bed of a man whose eyes have shrunk in their sockets. The Queen waves from her seat at a polo match.

At last Alex comes to a photograph of a wizened, square-faced woman. She wears an aquamarine silk scarf knotted at the throat, and simple pearl earrings. Her milky blue eyes squint forthrightly at the camera. She resembles very closely, Ana realizes with a start, Johnny's person.

"And Princess Alice," Alex says breathlessly, sliding an olive hand across the shiny paper. "Have you heard of Princess Alice, Duchess of Gloucester?"

"My mother looks like Isabel Preysler, from *Hola,*" Ana volunteers.

*   *   *

The desert sky is the color of a bruise. A handful of stars, widely scattered, wink faintly. From the window of her balcony Ana can see the city and the camel's-back mountain, a gray-brown hulk in the distance. She opens the minibar and takes out a doll-sized bottle of tequila. JOSE CUERVO, it says. HECHO EN MEXICO. She lights a cigarette from the pack her mother has forgotten on the night table. It tastes, as always, like fouled, muddied sand. She pours herself a tumbler of tequila and knocks it back in three gulps without wincing. She holds the cigarette in her teeth. "That's all right," she tells the mirror, "this stuff tastes better from a hookah."

She starts up the jacuzzi and pours in an entire bottle of bubble bath. She makes castles, stalagmites. She sculpts herself a party dress and waltzes across the tiles. She does a plié, an arabesque in front of the sink.

She leaves the shower faucet running and tells the room service waiter that her mother is in the bathroom. As she lets the pecan pie filling melt in her mouth like clear pudding, sips her warm

Cherry Coke, and later, as she spears her french fries and pushes them through a pool of ketchup, Ana decides that her mother really does look like Isabel Preysler: a petite sculpted face, shoulder-length chocolate hair, skirts that fall neatly, just above the knee. Isabel Preysler was once married to Julio Iglesias, which Ana finds as improbable as her mother's having been married to her father.

She thinks of the restaurant, the one on the seventh floor where the old men wore dark suits and the women who were not Japanese were blonde, their hair swept up and sprayed, like Princess Di's. There was a view. The waiters brought Ana and her mother mock turtle soup, lobster medallions, fluffy salads of rose petals, nasturtium, frills of chickory in a hazelnut vinaigrette, each plate sheltered under a pewter dome. The domes had tiny knobs on their tops, shaped like pineapples, a strawberry, a pear.

"*Voilà,*" the waiter would say, each time.

She had seen Alex and the troll-eyed man sitting along the back wall of the restaurant, squeezed into a purple banquette, under a teardrop chandelier. They looked out at the stars; they watched an airplane fly towards the north. They had ordered an entire vanilla cake. A waiter wheeled it to their table on a glass-paneled cart.

Her Cherry Coke needs ice. But when she thinks of going down to the second floor to the ice machine she has a sudden intuition that she would meet the troll-eyed man, still in his zebra stripe bikini, his flabby gray arms rooting in the bin. Or he might be standing pressed up next to the machine, not necessarily waiting for ice. Moths would flail against the overhead lamp. The maids would be in their sad little apartments, bus stops away. Alex would be in the disco.

Ana bolts the door and draws the chain. She swathes herself in a towel and goes out onto the balcony. The stars twinkle fiercely in the chill. The iron railing is nearly as cold as the tiny bottle of tequila. She drops the bottle over the side, into the thicket of palm, ivy, and fern.

She wraps her hands around the railing, arches her back. A breath of breeze sweeps her hair off her forehead; she lifts her chin.

The grass stretches below like an abyss, ringed by the spotlit path. Clusters of saguaro reach their thick arms to the stars. Near Johnny's house, she can make out a sand trap, dark like a wound. Beyond the grass is the highway. And beyond the highway is the city, shining now like a wonderland.

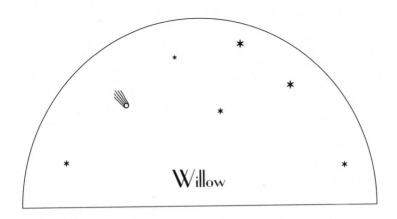

Willow

The name of my godchild was Willow. Her mother, my friend, is Zoe Rainbow, née Wilkins. I sent this godchild a birthday present for five straight years, Federal Express. When Willow was born, hand-knit booties. Then: a bib; a blanket; a stuffed rabbit; a set of pink plastic blocks; a Sleeping Beauty wristwatch. In that order.

Zoe has been my friend since we were in the Lewis Mather School in Chicago. Zoe moved to a small town two hours northwest of Madison, Wisconsin, some time ago. She doesn't drive; I had a lot of work. I really had a lot of work. So we hadn't seen each other since before this godchild Willow was born—since before, in fact, Zoe had gotten pregnant, by accident, by someone named Peter Rainbow who was a potter from Vermont, or a weaver from New Hampshire. Or maybe he was a carpenter from Oregon. This Peter person left Zoe when she was seven months pregnant (he joined the Peace Corps and went to Togo, or maybe it was Tonga) and Zoe called me from her little town two hours northwest of Madison and cried, and I called her back from New York so she could save money on her phone bill, and she cried. And then the baby cried. Then Zoe stopped calling me, although she invited me to be godmother (via postcard), and she sent me Christmas cards. For a few years anyway.

The first Christmas card had a photograph of Zoe and the baby both dressed as elves. The Christmas tree in the background looked like a weed. HAPPY HOLIDAYS, it hollered in fat red letters, AND SAVE THE PLANET. They looked crazed. Next Christmas, the baby's sitting on a goat, because, as Zoe's scrawl informed me, they were living with Reginald ("who's just the greatest most lovin' guy") and herding goats.

Since when did I have friends who would say "lovin'"? Since when did I have friends who herded goats? Since then. Since then, because people change, you know, your friends change, you go with them, you bend, you don't break. I sell Latin bonds. I wear Italian flats with little grosgrain bows. (I couldn't give a bugfuck about the planet.) I was this child's godmother.

Next Christmas, there's another baby, no Reginald, no goats, and everyone looks like they need to have their hair untangled. Then, nothing. For four years, nothing. But I sent Willow her birthday presents: a blanket; a stuffed rabbit; a set of pink plastic blocks; a Sleeping Beauty wristwatch. I wrapped them carefully with embossed paper and multicolored ribbon, thinking of how Willow would pull the bow apart, tear off the paper, fling it across the living room floor. Smile. Aunt Karen!

May 28, 1994, would have been Willow's sixth birthday. That week I had to fly to Chicago. And so I thought: why not rent a car? A few hours' drive. "Zoe? How are you?" "Oh, I'm fine." It went like that. Zoe sounded like she could have been next door. "And Willow?" "The kids are all so big now!" Good, I thought, good. I've always hated the squall of little children. Mommy this, Mommy that, felt-tip pen anywhere near your cream-colored slacks. Maybe they'll stay outside playing dodgeball or something.

But what kids? Who were all these big kids? Willow at six and that baby? Well, now Zoe was living with someone named Ted, who had three boys, Greg, John, Joe, or maybe it was Hal, Joe and John, their names swam around like tadpoles in my head. Ted made cheese because he had to, and he wrote poetry because he was a totally amazing genius.

"Poetry, what kind of poetry?"

"Ted's a *nature* poet."

"Nature like the little wildflowers and the wind and the whales?" I'd had a hard time, you know, with the goats.

"Nature is cruel. That kind of nature."

"Oh," I said. "Is Ted cruel?"

But I wanted to like this Ted, suddenly. And I wanted Ted to like me, to say to Zoe sometime at night, when they were under the covers, "That friend of yours, Karen, she's a really good friend." Zoe would snuggle closer and rest her head of black curls on his shoulder. "Oh Ted," she'd sigh, "you are so right."

I knew this was ridiculous. But I wanted Zoe to care about what I was doing now—I wanted to be able to tell her about my promotion to Vice President, about my new apartment in a building with a swimming pool overlooking Central Park. I wanted to be able to slip my shoes off, sprawl on her sofa (plum-colored, overstuffed?), feet up on the coffee table (a hand-painted pine chest?), and tell her this plan I have to set up a portfolio management company and run it from Boston. ("You could water your plants," she might laugh. "You might keep a cat now . . . cup of tea?")

And I wanted her to have told Willow about her godmother, and for Willow to want to sit next to me on the sofa, let me touch her hair—would it be long, so I could braid it for her? She would tell me the names of her dolls and the stuffed rabbit. She might show me her smudgy fingerpaintings, lumpy clay ashtrays from art class, ladybugs in a jar.

* * *

I stayed in Chicago two nights, at the Drake, the Drake by the lake. (There's a ditty about that I used to know.) On the first day, after I made my presentation, I stopped by the Water Tower shopping mall and bought Willow a life-sized baby doll. It could wee-wee if you pushed its belly button. It could say, "Mommy I love you," and if you switched a knob on the small of its back, "Hold me tight." Its eyes were blueberry blue.

I imagined Willow combing out its stiff yellow curls, tucking it into a little bed, next to the rabbit. She'd be wearing her Sleeping Beauty wristwatch. Her pink blocks would be strewn across the carpet. She might kneel beside the little bed and sing a made-up song:

> *Little baby don't you weep*
> *Hush now baby go to sleep*

Or she might hate the doll. Or she might already have one just like it. Or maybe it would get lost or stolen. I imagined the doll dirty, missing an arm, face down on a pile of old newspapers.

Enough, I told myself. Enough.

I decided the doll looked like a Linda, or a Lorrie. Or a Lulu: *Lulu with your eyes so blue.* I took it back to my hotel room and sat it on the armchair by the window. Then I met my clients for dinner.

I was trying to sell them a Mexican Eurobond, fully collateralized, with semiannual variable interest payments, two full basis points above Treasuries. This was the kind of bond, the kind of low risk high yield, I said for the third time that day, that makes you sorry when it matures.

"It's slim pickings out there," I said.

"That's not been our experience," said the one who looked like the youngest boy on "The Brady Bunch." He wasn't more than a year or two out of Harvard Business School. He sliced his seared ahi in gingered lime sauce. He said, "We've been getting some extraordinary yields in Indonesia."

"Yeah, and Kuala Lumpur." The other one reminded me of Dennis the Menace. He had a Ph.D. in operations research. "We're cleaning up with palm oil futures," he said.

When he set his espresso cup down for the last time, Brady Bunch said, "I don't know about Mexico. Just when you think its economy is chugging along fine, it goes over a cliff."

"Poof," the other one said, and threw his napkin up in the air.

"Good old Me-hico," Brady Bunch said, dreamily, leaning back in his chair. Now that I'd paid the check, I knew he was going to launch into a reminiscence about his last trip to Zihuatanejo with his girlfriend, and how great the margaritas are at the Villa del Sol.

These guys always do that.

I came back to my room to find the doll tucked into the bed, its eyes closed. I was confused for a minute; then I spied two tiny foil-wrapped mints, one on each pillow. It gave me a start to realize the maid must have thought I was traveling with a child.

* * *

"I will *never* have kids." That's what I said to Zoe the last afternoon we played hooky. I remember drinking Cokes, then pushing through the Drake's brass revolving doors, our noses held high (ready to insist that our grandmother was staying in room number 126) so we could use the ladies room. Earlier that afternoon we had wandered through Marshall Field's department store, touching the racks of silk blouses, mohair sweaters. "Oh I *want* that," Zoe would say, pulling out a sleeve and pressing it to her cheek. "I *want* that."

"Why don't you just take it?" I had dared her.

At twilight we were on the Oak Street Beach, smoking cigarettes, pretending to inhale. It was early fall and the churning water was dull. The wind whipped our hair and smoke behind us. We stubbed out the butts in the sand, and lit up again, and again. We buried our feet, rained handfuls of sand over our knees. The sand was cool, but dry and warm once it was on our legs. We drew deep circles and spirals with our fingertips. We were talking about our husbands, what they would be like. Zoe's was going to be six feet tall with hair the color of hazelnut shells. He would play "Stairway to Heaven" on the guitar, he would be a botanist, he would be a potter, he would have a shop that sold herbs, or handmade furniture, or bongs. They would have ten children, five boys and five girls. They would live on a farm and ride dappled Arabians.

I was going to marry a movie producer. Or a plastic surgeon with a practice on Park Avenue. I was going to live in New York City and be a famous painter, like Elaine de Kooning—but I only said that because we'd seen Elaine de Kooning's photograph in a magazine. The painter was perched on a stool, her tiny triangle of a chin in one hand. She was smoking. (I was smoking. But I had a big square chin.)

It seemed so sudden the way the sky had fallen over the lake, like an immense shroud. A trawler anchored a few miles out glittered in the chill.

"I wonder if we could swim out to that," I said, just to keep the conversation going.

"No we couldn't," Zoe said.

"I could swim out to that," I said.

"Don't be stupid," Zoe said, and chucked her half-smoked cigarette out into the surf.

We sat there for a while, too annoyed with each other to speak.

Then Zoe pulled something out of her backpack and gently placed it around my shoulders. It was an Extra Large charcoal gray mohair sweater with mother-of-pearl buttons. I could feel their cold unevenness between my fingers.

I still have that sweater, folded in my wardrobe, stuffed with mothballs.

It's funny though, whenever I think of that twilight on the beach I see us as if from far out from shore, hovering just above the lake. We are small girls, our thin arms hugging our knees. We are sitting far apart, although the beach is deserted. The city is ablaze behind us.

* * *

Not long after, we were expelled from the Lewis Mather School, which was a relief for all parties concerned, except our parents. My mother blamed it on Zoe; my father was in a coma, literally.

"There were forty-two other girls in your class. *Forty-two,*" my mother had said, as if it were a magic number, and more than plenty for the money.

I was sent to a boarding school in Connecticut where I had to stop smoking. I played field hockey and began to do well in math, of all things. Zoe was sent to the Lab School in Hyde Park. She started to smoke pot, and she fell in with a different crowd, boys who had long frizzy hair and wore Guatemalan sandals. I approved completely: we were both *persona non grata* with everyone from Lewis Mather. We'd always had that much in common.

We would see each other on vacations, for a day or so, before Zoe would have to go with her parents wherever they went: Ireland, a cruise to view the glaciers on the Alaska coast, Barbados. We'd share a joint at Lincoln Park, then take the bus down to the Water Tower and wander through the cosmetics department at Marshall Field's or Lord and Taylor's, trying on lipsticks, spritzing ourselves with Halston and Diorissimo, giggling like idiots. Then we'd find a bench

outside the McDonald's on the top floor and pig-out on raspberry
Frango mints.

If we saw any of our old classmates we'd pretend we didn't know
them. We never saw any of the teachers, except once, when we saw
our old American History teacher, Mrs. Negelbaum. She was riding
up the escalator towards the mezzanine of the mall and we passed her,
riding down. She was holding an enormous shopping bag against her
stomach. She looked right through us, then with the slightest twitch
under one cheek, she fixed her stare at the back of the man in front
of her.

∗ ∗ ∗

In all these years since then there's been only one time anyone else
from Lewis Mather saw me, that I know of. It was a few days before
I had to go to Chicago, in a grocery store near my apartment. I was
pushing a cart down the frozen food aisle when a woman just behind
me cried, "Karen? Karen!" I kept going—fish sticks, chicken nuggets,
Chinese whatnots for the microwave. My name is so common, when
I turn around it's always a stranger waving at someone else.

"Karen! It's me, Susan Powell!" A red-haired woman with a face
as round and scrubbed as a new potato had pulled her cart up along-
side mine, and she was blinking at me as if she had a tic. She
looked vaguely familiar—the freckles across her nose looked right,
her pudgy hands, modest pearl-drop earrings.

"Karen from Lewis Mather! Don't you remember me?"

I arranged my face into a smile, but I didn't have a clue who this
woman was.

"I was in Mr. O'Higgins's Spanish class with you! And I was in
Mrs. Strauss's Trigonometry class with you and Zoe!" She was still
blinking. "You and Zoe Wilkins, remember? You sat right in front
of me!"

"Oh," I said. "What did you say your name was?"

"Susan Powell. I'm Cindy Powell's sister?"

I had the fleeting hope I might have changed enough (my skin had cleared up, I was wearing contact lenses, I'd had my chin fixed) to claim that this had all been a mistake, that I was named Karen, yes, but I'd never gone to the Lewis Mather School, that I was in fact from L.A., or Philadelphia, or Toronto. Anywhere.

"I was on the tennis team with Zoe," the woman was burbling. "Remember? We went to a tournament in Lake Forest and Zoe cut everyone's racquet strings with a razor?" She had begun to giggle, holding her hand over her breast. "You and Zoe, Karen and Zoe, oh God. I never thought I'd ever lay eyes on you again!"

"Well, here I am."

She blinked and cocked her head. "And how are you? I mean, what have you been doing? After, you know . . . where did you go?"

She was wearing plaid shorts and flat-heeled Italian sandals. Her hair was sprayed. I just couldn't place her. Susan Powell, Susan Powell. I told her my life story anyway, standing there in an aisle of Metropolitan Foods.

* * *

I was up at daybreak on Saturday, May 28, 1994. My garment bag was packed, my teeth were brushed. I pushed up the window and watched the sun rise over the lake like an enormous yolk, spilling out along the horizon. The air felt light, shot with possibility. The traffic was still so thin I could hear each truck, each car as it shifted gears and came around the curve of the shore. Birds were singing somewhere. I looked down at the beach below, but there was only a stooped black figure, a bag lady? The water was calm and intensely blue.

Fifteen minutes later I was heading north on Shoreline Drive in my rental car, the air-conditioning on high, humming along with the radio. Zoe, I was going to see Zoe. I was finally going to meet this child, my godchild Willow. The Willow I had sent birthday presents to every year. A bib, a blanket, a stuffed rabbit . . . I had the doll next to me on the front seat. Lulu, I had decided.

"Willow," I would say with my fairy godmother voice, "this is your new doll Lulu."

"Lulu." Willow would smile shyly and hug it to her chest.

Or she might say, "No. That's not her name," and look at me suspiciously.

But it is, I thought. Her name is Lulu. How awful that she might be something else, that her entire doll-destiny was to be called Linda, or Jacey. Or Nicole. Left on a shelf with the other forgotten toys. Shut in a box and locked in the basement. I looked at Lulu sitting next to me in the passenger seat. Her blueberry eyes were wide open, staring at the glove compartment.

Enough.

And suddenly I realized: I had forgotten to buy a present for Zoe. I was going to be Zoe's houseguest, if only for one night. But I was a long way out of Chicago by then. When I came to a cluster of Howard Johnson, Burger King, Shell, I turned off the interstate and headed west. I passed tract houses, a baseball diamond, a church with a white steeple. I drove by lush green cornfields, soybean fields, clapboard houses fenced with windswept trees. A calf lay bloated on the shoulder, a smear of crimson across the road. What had I expected? There wouldn't be anything to buy out here. But just as I was about to make a U-turn, I saw a roadside stand selling cherries.

Then I was back on the interstate, a gallon jar of cherry preserves propped up on the passenger seat next to Lulu. "Isn't that sweet?" I said, tapping the square of calico on the lid of the jar. I hadn't slept enough; I was feeling light-headed. I decided to stop in Madison for a donut and several cups of coffee.

* * *

I recognized the capitol. It was hard to miss, standing on a hill in the center of the city gleaming whiter than marble in the morning sun. But it seemed incredible that I'd been here before: the trees were thick now with waxy leaves; and yellow and red tulips, their buds tight and small, were everywhere—massed in front of the buildings, into the medians, along the parking strips, in clay pots on the sidewalks in front of the shops. The sidewalks were filled with students walking alone, or in groups of two or three. Most, even the girls, were wearing oversized shirts and baseball caps thrown on backwards. Their faces seemed so unformed, much too young for university, for life.

I'd been in Madison at the end of November 1980, when Zoe was finishing her first and only semester at the University of Wisconsin. She was majoring in biology because, she said, she was going to be a pediatrician. I was at the University of Chicago, about to major in astrophysics. It was the Thanksgiving weekend. My father was not in a coma anymore; he was dead.

Zoe was living in a dorm room with two other girls, Sally and Tracy. Tracy was from Appleton, I remember that. Sally was going to join a sorority, Phi Kappa Zappa, Zappa Kappa Tao. Sally and Tracy were blonde and thin-boned. They smoked menthols. They wore watermelon lip gloss. (If they'd lived in Chicago, they would have gone to Lewis Mather.) They left to eat turkey and watch football with their parents.

Zoe slammed the door after them. "Ha!" she laughed in a theatrical whisper, and threw herself on her bed. Her black hair had grown so long it trailed on the linoleum floor. I noticed her textbooks lying under the bed behind a line of dust bunnies.

"What?" I said.

"I'm sleeping with her boyfriend, that's what." And she grabbed her stomach and went into peals of laughter.

"Whose boyfriend?"

"Tracy's. His name is Adalberto." She had said this like *Ah-dahll-bare-toe.* More laughter.

"Adalberto," I said, feeling the syllables roll off my tongue. I'd never even kissed anybody.

"His parents are from Cuba. We spent last weekend in Chicago. We drank champagne at the top of the John Hancock."

I was impressed. "But he doesn't sound like your type," I said.

"He's not," Zoe said, and rolled over onto her stomach, her bare feet waggling in the air. She'd painted her toenails parsley green. She twisted her hair into a rope, flung it behind her shoulder, propped herself up on one elbow, and pulled a bag of sinsemilla out of the back pocket of her jeans. It was all a single sinuous motion.

"I've got to do a problem set," I said. "Plus read a ton of stuff before Monday." I'd already bitten all my fingernails to the quick on the bus.

She trickled a pinch of the grass into a bong then struck a match. "Well," she said. Her eyes were small and bloodshot. "If it isn't Elaine the Conehead."

I wasn't sure what she meant by that. I shrugged. "I never could paint," I said. (Actually, I'd never tried.) The bong was bubbling loudly now and the room had begun to stink of burning pine sap. I watched her take a hit, then hold it in, puckering her face, clenching her shoulders. She exhaled.

"But you're good at math."

"Yeah," I said. My eyes had started to smart. I put on my coat.

"The library's closed," she said. She passed me the bong.

I'd already taken out my homework and was considering the first problem: *A body moves at a constant speed in a perfectly circular path. What are the forces that are present or absent in this system?* That wasn't too tough.

I inhaled, deeply.

The only other thing I remember about that weekend was the snow. It began just after midnight, falling straight and thick. I stood with Zoe at the window and watched it blanket the lamplights, the grass, the winding pathway to the library. I might have said something about our oneness with the hydrogen atoms, the unseen planets circling distant stars, the Magellanic Clouds. We usually laughed ourselves silly when we smoked, but this time we just stood there with our elbows on the cold tile ledge, our breath fogging the glass. But there wasn't anything unusual about the snow, or the view.

* * *

Not long after, Zoe dropped out of school. We lost touch for a few years. I graduated, went to business school in Boston, then moved to Manhattan. I began to travel in my work: Panama, London, Buenos Aires. I lived in Mexico City for six months. My mother remarried and moved to a suburb of Seattle. Then Zoe called to tell me about Peter, who had left. And then there was Willow. There was always, although I had never met her, never heard her voice, my godchild Willow.

Willow, I was thinking when I went through a red light and sideswiped a school bus. No one was in it but the driver. I tore part of my right fender off and the jar of cherry preserves broke on the floor. Lulu landed face down in the goo.

Later, after the police came, after I got another rental car, I called Zoe.

"Yep?" Ah, Ted the cheesemaker poet.

"It's Karen."

"Yep."

"Is this Ted?"

"Yep."

"Listen, I'm on my way for Willow's birthday, but I've had an accident, I'm OK, the car's OK, well, it's a rental car, you know, they gave me another one, just a fender bender actually, but, um . . . hello?"

"Yep."

"I'll be late, I have—"

"Zoe!" The receiver clunked down and I heard Ted shouting for her to come to the phone. I waited for what seemed to be (but probably were not) several minutes. I could hear a small child crying, a dog barking, and then the low rattle of a motor, like a lawnmower revving up, or a drill.

Finally, someone hung up the phone.

* * *

The sky had nothing in it but the sun, and it was still low, behind the capitol. I walked out of the phone booth into this impossible profusion of flowers and child-like faces, pizza restaurants, coffee shops, used bookstores, video arcades.

A rollerblader whizzed by me, grazing my shoulder with her glove. How many years had it been?

* * *

I don't know why, but I thought of the time I saw Tracy. I felt a sense of vertigo to realize it must have been eleven years ago. She was coming out of the McDonald's on Michigan Avenue with a boy who was wearing a University of Wisconsin sweatshirt. He was short and slight, but his hair was an ashy blonde. So much for Adalberto, I thought.

But later, when I went into Latin bonds, when I lived in Mexico

City, I worked with men whose names were García Vega, Romero, López Villalpando, and they were blonde. They wore expensive wire-rimmed glasses. Sometimes, on Saturdays, their wives would let them take their children to the McDonald's on the Periferico. They always ordered something called a *caja féliz*, a hamburger with fries, I imagine.

* * *

Two hours and ten minutes later I pulled up to Zoe's house. It was a Victorian three-story painted cream. In the driveway three teenage boys were playing basketball. Greg, Hal, Glenn? Hal, John, Joe? A new Volkswagen minivan was parked in the driveway. The lawn had been neatly mowed and there was a cherry tree laden with fruit in its center. A lone crow pecked at the cherries that had fallen around the trunk.

Oh, my gallon jar of preserves had been all wrong.

"Karen!" It was Ted, calling me from where he sat in a straight-backed rocking chair on the porch. He had big hands and a smooth face (which surprised me). But his hair had streaks of silver and his nose was too small. He was wearing jeans and a blue work shirt. The black labrador lying next to him lifted its muzzle and looked at me as if to say, And?

I waved and started across the grass, holding Lulu on my hip.

"Karen!" His voice was soft, but sharp. Like goat cheese. He stood up and moved slowly towards me as if something pained him. The three boys looked at him sullenly, and one of them slammed the ball against the garage door. Then the boys filed into the house.

Ted took my arm and led me to a rocking chair. There were several of them lined up across the porch, maybe five or six. I sat down and rocked backwards. I rocked forward. The runners made a noise on the floor like a metal ball spiraling down a chute. Ted sat down so carefully his chair could have been nailed to the planks. He shoved his hands into his pockets. He looked away, at the tree. "Willy's dead," he blurted. "Four years ago." He coughed.

I stopped rocking. I had wiped the doll's face with a Handywipe and now it smelled, slightly, of alcohol and detergent. I hadn't realized how badly stained its hair was. My hands made fists around its arms, which were hard, hard as stone. I don't know where my voice came from.

I said: "You called her Willy."

I think I had wanted that to be a question. But of course, it was not a question. I had nothing to ask Ted. I stood up, holding the doll as if it were a weapon. I started for Zoe's front door.

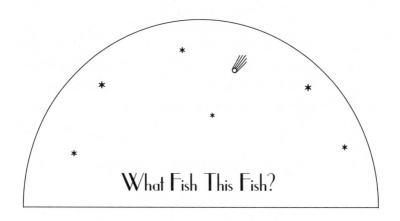

What Fish This Fish?

They owe me everything.
Mobutu Sese Seko Kuku Ngbendu wa za Banga

Rail links between the towns have disappeared beneath the encroaching jungle. The sun is a cinnamon disk on the lake. A flamingo takes flight, its legs dangling like broken twigs. There is a faint *clack-tink-clack* from a mobile kitchen behind the veranda as a servant stirs ice into our drinks. These would be green drinks, artificial limeade trucked in from the foreign-exchange-only store perhaps. Freshly sprayed insecticide stings our nostrils, our lips, the rims of our eyelids. Mr. Bob has his hands wrapped around the gold-flecked arms of his fiberglass throne. His eyes are bloodshot, his pupils dilated. I am sure his palms are sweaty. It seems Mr. Bob would have his palms stick to his throne, hard. Then he might squinch them off and hold them out to me, a-sparkle with gold leaf. My name is Evan Stevens. I work for the G-7 Bank.

"Mr. Evan," Mr. Bob says. There is a quaver in his voice, a tilt to his neck, a cringe in his wishbone shoulders. I wave my hand through the empty air. I mean to indicate there, beyond the veranda, the marble patio where the bodyguards finger their Chinese submachine guns. I mean to indicate the encroaching jungle, the black Mercedes, the kennels, the deep freeze (for steaks) the size of a Jack-N-the-Box drive-in. But there is no steak left.

"Mr. Evan," Mr. Bob says, a smile cracking his face, "why you wave now? They just spray here."

I laugh. The servant brings me a green drink in a Baccarat tumbler. It sweats cold in my palm. "You need a fiscal adjustment," I say. "The problem is sweet potatoes."

In fact, the problem is many problems. The problem is Mr. Bob's Luxembourgeois bank accounts, but not only that: the fleet of army trucks (stranded on the other side of the lake for lack of spare parts), the Mr. Bob convention center–shopping–hotel complex (completed in time for the Pan-Central Conference of Nations, but without plumbing), Mr. Bob's third wife's sons' television company. Not to mention the 17,655 bureaucrats who have worked without pay for the last month. Or the soldiers. Or the bodyguards. I wonder if they have any bullets left for their guns.

Mr. Bob is going to have to export 73 percent of the sweet potato crop, according to my calculations.

"Is possible," Mr. Bob says, brushing something off the front of his gray sharkskin suit, "to become paralyzed by eating too many sweet potatoes."

I know this. Sweet potatoes have traces of cyanide. Yet one would have to eat nothing, nothing but sweet potatoes for about three months before one might, might begin to feel a weakness in the joints. But this is irrelevant. The sweet potato is this country's staple crop.

The air is very still. Shadows are looming larger now behind the throne, the potted bamboo, the filing cabinets on wheels. A dog barks, weakly, almost a whine. There is a sudden rustling in the dead grasses along the shore. One of the bodyguards aims his submachine gun at the noise. His skin looks sallow, yellow. It has—yes—a tinge of pumpkin. (Which reminds me of Miss Frietchie, my seventh-grade science teacher. After she got divorced, she went on a diet and ate nothing but tomatoes and carrots for two months. The PTA made her take a blood test to prove she did not have hepatitis.)

My drink is not limeade. It tastes of corn syrup. Of food dye. I decide not to retch.

"It's your sole source of foreign exchange right now," I say. "We'll be forced to cut you off otherwise." The dog emerges from the grass. Its ribs protrude. It has a small flamingo in its jaws. As it pads towards the veranda, the bird's twig-like legs drag along the dirt.

"Sweet potatoes with spring onion and chile," Mr. Bob says. He knocks back his green drink. "Sweet potatoes with apple blossom honey and Devonshire cream." He screws up his eyes and his face cracks again. His fists are clenched in his lap. "Sweet potatoes cut up into cubes and deep-fried in dog fat."

Pop. Pop-pop-pop.

The bodyguard has shot the dog. Mr. Bob whips out his sunglasses. He settles the gold shafts over his ears and sits back again, his hands wrapped around the arms of his throne. His face is so small. He looks like he has fly eyes.

"Seventy-three percent should do it," I say. I set my Baccarat tumbler down on the filing cabinet. "We can put you in contact with Save the Children." I cough, cough up nothing.

The rim of my Baccarat tumbler is solid black with gnats.

"Remoras!" Mr. Bob shouts. "Remoras!"

Perhaps this is the name of the servant, because he comes running in from the mobile kitchen with a frantic look on his face. Mr. Bob points at my drink. The servant pulls a rusted can out of his apron pocket and sprays directly into my glass. The nozzle begins spitting; the servant shakes the can viciously. "*No hay,*" There isn't any, he says with his eyes pale and round. "*No hay.*" The spray has left a film like gasoline. The servant does not remove my drink. And in a moment, the gnats come back, harder to see now in the twilight. I scratch a welt on the web of skin between my thumb and index finger.

"You've got to get your current account back into surplus," I say, recrossing my legs, brushing my cheek. (Fortunately, the insect repellant I picked up in London is fairly strong.) "You can't take the figures your Minister of Finance gives you—" I should be diplomatic, I've been told to remember to try to be diplomatic, but what the hell. "His figures are wildly off the mark. You have a current account deficit of 1.72 billion U.S. Dollars, according to G-7 Bank calculations."

"Refresh my memory," Mr. Bob says, his palms pressed flat on the arms of his throne. "What is current account?"

The sky is livid now, but the lake is gunmetal, calm. A chorus has started up: *chlurrr-chlurrr, rikki-rika-rika, rikki-rika-rika.* The bamboo shivers, drops a slender leaf. I open my briefcase and take out a pen and pad of paper. "You've got your balance of payments," I say, writing almost blindly, screwing up my eyes in the dim. "A., you've got your capital account, which records all the investments and credits from foreigners, minus all the money you send abroad. B., you've got your current account, which records all the goods and services you export, minus all the goods and services you import." Something bites me on the chin.

"Mr. Evan, pardon me?"

"The current account records all the goods and services you export, minus—" *Rika-rika-chlurrr.*

Mr. Bob has been served a bowl of chopped fish. He is using his fingers to pick out chunks with the scales still stuck to one side, and swallowing them whole.

There is no moon. The sky is a shroud of heat, pinpricked with stars. Mr. Bob has not taken off his sunglasses.

"Remora." He holds the bowl out to me. I shake my head, no; I've already emptied two bottles of Pepto-Bismol.

The din of insects is almost deafening, but I can hear the servant cranking up the generator. It sputters, and overhead a rice paper lantern flickers on, then off.

"We have no longer gasoline," Mr. Bob shouts at me. The servant carries in a tray of Baccarat candleholders with rolled beeswax candles in them. As he sets them down, the flames lick towards his cheeks, the yellows of his eyes. Mr. Bob leans forward, an elbow on a knee. His teeth are abnormally long, perfectly straight.

"We have no longer Minister of Finance," he shouts, and his laugh goes off like a volcano. *Chlurrr.* Still breathing heavily, Mr. Bob takes off his glasses and wanders his stare over my face, my neck, my hair. His skin is furred with mosquitoes. He doesn't slap himself. He lifts a finger and a bodyguard clomps up and stands directly behind my chair. I can smell him: fresh sweat and sandalwood aftershave. So young. Laundered cotton.

Suddenly, there is quiet. Something splashes in the lake.

"Tell Mr. Evan what is remora." The gold flecks leap from the fiberglass with the candlelight.

"Remora is a fish. Sir." I can feel the bodyguard's warm breath on my neck.

"Tell Mr. Evan what fish this fish."

"Remora is little fish that sucks on sharks. Sir."

Rik.

I reach down into my briefcase and pull out my cellular phone. I punch the number, the G-7 Bank jeep is on the way. Mr. Bob has thrown his bowl on the floor. In the flicker of candlelight I can see the scales shining. I can see the bloodshot of his eyes. And he begins to slap himself on the throat, his wrists, the back of his hands, his cheeks, chin, nape, temples.

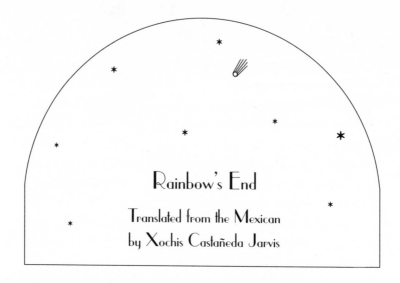

Rainbow's End

Translated from the Mexican
by Xochis Castañeda Jarvis

"*You're the top,*" Chabela sings in my ear, sweet and soft.
"*You're the top!*
You're the Colosseum.
You're the top!
You're the Louvre Museum . . ."
Then she holds my hand and clacks her wedding band against mine
and she sings, "*You're the Empire State Building*" and "*You're a Mont
Blanc pen*" or a "*Hermès tie*" and "*You're the best linguini with four cheeses
at the Café des Artistes.*"

Later I realize she didn't make all that stuff up. She took me once
to a club in New York where this chubby little Negro pounded the
keys and sang it. Bobby Snort or something. You know, everybody's
drinking Chivas and acting sophisticated. Smoky little room with a
big cover charge. But most of it—*You're a Mont Blanc pen, a Hermès*

Xochis (aka Roberto Anastasio) Castañeda Jarvis is a cross-dresser who designs price-hedging
strategies using futures and options for a coffee interest based in Xalapa. She (he) is not personally
acquainted with the narrator, one Juventino Pérez López; however, Xochis has read all about him
in the Mexico City newspapers, as have we all.

tie, linguini, ha—Chabela made that up. But that's why I like her, see. She's sweet and romantic-like.

Sometimes. Sometimes she's sweet and romantic-like. Depends. Every six months she gets her collagen injections. And just before she goes to the clinic in La Jolla, she starts tearing out magazine articles. Face-lifts. Electrolysis. Liposuction. I don't know what for— she looks forty-two going on twenty-six. Puts her in a bad mood. We're talkin' jewelry. Furniture. Decorator fabrics.

She sings to me, la de da de da, and then, if she thinks I'm not gonna give her what she wants, she ends up with *"You're the bottom, I'm the top!"* Well, it's supposed to go, *"If I'm the bottom, you're the top!"* And now we're in month number five and she's singing me this business all day long. I can see that I'm gonna have a problem.

And I already got problems. I'm married to her.

Exhibit A: Her kid, Chabelita. Carbon copy. Fourteen and doesn't miss a thing. Just like the grandmother, Josefina, that rabid old possum. HEY. That's the TRUTH. Couldn't stand her. Always judging. Josefina liked me, though, I could tell. But that was because of my money and because it was an easy act to follow Chabela's last two husbands. First one, he's some kind of alcoholic. Handsome though. I saw an old photo album once, of their wedding. He looked like Pedro Armendáriz, the guy in all those Dolores Del Río, María Félix movies—or Clark Gable, but his ears don't stick out. Me, I'm an ugly sonofabitch from the Gulf. Josefina, the white queen of the fuckin' world, she called me a *naco* behind my back. Well, I AM a *naco.* But I got money, more of it than Josefina ever saw, even when she was a kid, when her father was doing all this business with the French. So he makes a bank (and the way Josefina went on about it you'd never know it got nationalized), and he builds a French-style house stuffed full of fancy junk. They even got plaster putti—yeah, poo-tee—fat little buggers, stuck all over the ceilings. And those dusty old rugs Chabela keeps yammering about. She wanted one of them Aubussons her brother sold after Josefina died, I could tell. Chabela's face twitches whenever she gets real mad. We're sitting at dinner chomping on those tinned cookies they buy at the Palacio de Hierro goor-may section and the brother says, "I got a good deal on the carpets."

I go, "Whad'ya get, Victor?"

Talking about money is just so, you know.

"A substantial amount," he says, sniffy. And his eyes are burning coals. The kind you want to dump water on. I go, "Vik-ter, whad'ya get?"

"Three hundred thousand," he says. A piece of cookie falls in his lap. "Dollars."

Chabela's face just about twitches into a locked-in snit. But I say: GOOD THING. I'll be damned if I'm gonna put that kind of dirty old rag in my house. Now Chabela's gonna want me to buy her an Aubusson at auction in New York. HA! I can see that one coming all the way from Guanajuato. On a lame donkey in a cloud of dust.

Then the brother hands me a cigar and tells me I don't know what's what with cigars.

"Juvi," he says, "you think you can get everything and the best of everything in New York. But not these. These are Cuban—fresh from Fidel's plantations."

Me! He tells this to me! From Veracruz! What a clown.

"Rolled on the thighs of virgins," he says.

More like rolled on the armpit of some fat negrita with twelve kids. The only good cigars in this world are made in Veracruz. And that's a fuckin' FACT.

Then he wants investment advice. More like he wants to know where I get my money and where I'm gonna get more money. He thinks my brother the Governor lets me in on the action. But what he knows and what I'm gonna tell him are the same thing: nothin'. I just smiley. Smiley all the time, nice little *naco*. They never know what I'm really thinking, and they never know what I'm really doing.

I'm the top.

* * *

So it's February. We're in New York. We start as we usually do: spending money. We take a cab from the Mayfair to the Burberry's on 57th Street. So the air's a little nippy, the Platinum card's feeling hot, and I'm thinking we'll take a trip. Like maybe Poland. Tonight. Save myself three hundred thousand dollars and keep the floors decent.

So I say to Chabela and the kid, "How 'bout some new Burberry's coats?" Course, they always agree with everything I suggest when it comes to spending money, so we go in and we buy some coats. Nice wool and cashmere blends. A turquoise one for Chabela and a red one with a cape for the kid. Me? One hundred percent cashmere charcoal gray.

I'm a happy guy. I got my coats, I got my women, we're walking down the street and I just start thinking, where would you be without the money? Huh? Where'd you be? I think this a lot of course, but I'm just thinking it a little sharper, a little clearer than usual. Like the kid hates me, this ain't news, but there she is, prancing down Third Avenue in New York City in her new Burberry's coat, and Chabela, well, I don't know about Chabela, but there she is too, scheming and plotting to get me into that rug sale, and what do I see. We're right at the entrance to Bloomingdale's and I see a white guy, blonde! Skinny as hell, covered with sores, lying on a piece of cardboard on the sidewalk. He's under a ratty lookin' blanket and he's got a sign he wrote with black crayon that says:

help me please
I have aids
bless you

Chabela and the kid, they stand there in front of the revolving door, all these people coming in and out, the wind blowing colder, arguing about whether they should check out the Giorgio Armani boutique on the fourth floor or the sunglasses and scarves on the ground floor or should they just split up and we'll meet in an hour for tea at the Mayfair?

Well, I have to be honest and I have to tell you: these white guys always grab my ticker. I always think, you know, in the back of my mind, if you're white it's all A-OK. You're never going to be out there selling Chiclets with the Indians, gettin' jacked around by the police. And if you're a white American. WELL. Somebody looks at you funny, you just flash your passport and call in the fuckin' Marines. But here's another one of these guys. Uh-huh.

And I'm bored! I AM REALLY BORED. How many times have we come to New York? To Burberry's, to Bloomingdale's? And Gucci and Bijan and Her-meez and Trump Tower? How many times has Chabela had a facial at Elizabeth Arden? How many times has the kid gone riding in Central Park? How many times have we stayed at the Mayfair? Rented a limo to go to Broadway? *Cats, Layʒ Miʒ-er-ah-blayʒ, Phantom of the Opera.* All these trips to New York are the same. Same, same, SAME.

Chabela and the kid decide to start with Giorgio Armani and I stand there smiley smiley and say yup let's meet at the Mayfair at three for tea, and the revolving door goes *whoosh* and I just set down on my haunches like an Indian waiting for the bus and I say, "*What's your name, brother?*"

He doesn't answer. So I ask him again. "*What's your name? You got a name?*"

And all he does is open one yellow eye and look at me like a dog on a highway that just got run over.

So I pick him up. I'm a strong guy. HEY! I spent three years working in the cane fields. I pick him up, and throw him over my shoulder like a sack of rotten potatoes. He moans a little, and he smells like shit and piss and vomit and dried sweat.

But what are dry cleaners for?

I walk all the way up to Park Avenue and 65th and I walk into the Mayfair. Nobody says nothin'. NEW YORK! Nobody even looks at me. I walk past the giant flower thing in the middle of the lobby and I go up the elevator and into our suite and I unload this guy onto the sofa.

And I sit down in the armchair next to the sofa and I look at him— passed out, drooling on the upholstery.

* * *

It's not easy getting the clothes off someone who's passed out, but I do it. I put 'em in a plastic Mayfair laundry bag. I'm thinking I should chuck it out, stuff it in the can, but I think nah, let's see what the Mayfair laundry can do.

I give him a bath. I fill the tub, throw in some of that bath gel they give you in a little bottle, and let him soak for a while. I have to watch him though, 'cause his head keeps slipping down.

Then I towel him off, put him in the white terrycloth hotel robe, and set him back on the sofa.

I fix him up. I wipe off his nose, I comb his hair—with Chabelita's comb. I shave him. I toss a little Chanel Anteus aftershave on his cheeks and neck. And he don't look so bad. Well, he's pale and he needs a haircut and he's got sores all over—but not too many on his face.

"*Where am I?*" he says. He looks around the room, he touches the terrycloth robe, and he closes his eyes. Smiles.

I get him a glass of water. He's perking up now. He's drinking the water, sitting up, well, more or less, and he's looking at me. Sort of. I don't think his eyes are focusing. They're round and watery, like a baby's. He ain't gonna say nuthin', he's waiting for me to say something. I tell him the kid's gonna get him some clothes and then we'll all watch videos here in the room. And maybe order a couple of pizzas. Or Chinese food. *Godfather III* and Szechuan prawns. How does that sound?

"*Far out,*" he says.

Can you believe these Americans? FAR OUT.

* * *

At three I meet Chabela and the kid downstairs for tea. Tea! Me! I order a whiskey with soda and a piece of chocolate cake. They like all those funny little teas—early gray, orange peekyboo, that stuff. And all those funny little sahnd-whiches. They bring 'em to you three plates one on top of the other. Cucumber. Watercress. Ha! But the smoked salmon ones ain't so bad. Chabela always gives me hers.

"Gee, honey, you smell kind of strange." Chabela is checking her makeup in her little tortoiseshell mirror thing.

"Yeah," says the kid. "You smell like piss or something." Chabela looks at her sharp.

"I have a new friend," I say. "And until I cleaned him up, he smelled like piss. Definitely. Piss." I take a swig of the whiskey and soda. "And vomit and shit and sweat."

Chabela snaps it shut. Her face goes white. But the kid smiles.

Like a cat. I look at the new coats, turquoise and red, slung over the backs of their chairs. The linings are matching silk and they shine like jewels under the chandelier. I reach out and take Chabela's salmon sandwich. It's good with a squeeze of lemon, a bit of dill, and a couple of them green things.

"You know," I say with my mouth full, "the salmon is so much better in Poland. 'Specially in February."

And what is there to do but agree?

* * *

Back in the suite, my new friend is asleep on the sofa, wheezing, like his lungs are gurgling. Chabela and the kid act like he's not there. They toss their shopping bags in the corner, by the cabinet with the TV in it, throw their coats on the armchair.

They go in the bathroom. Shut the door. They get the water running, like they always do, so I can't hear what they're saying. First, Chabela's gonna complain about the scum in the tub. Then they're gonna have a fight. Like I care. I stand over the sofa with my arms crossed, checking out my friend. He looks OK, no problem, just looks like a kid who grew too fast—bones too big for his skin. Bad case of acne. I hear Chabelita say, "Ma moo mooo mamoo momoma HOSPI-TAL," and Chabela says, "Momo mooma WARSAW ma mo o." Then they turn on the bathtub.

I give him a shake on the shoulder, but no dice. So I pull him up, shove his legs over, and there he is! Sitting up on the sofa! SEHR GUT, Very good. But then his head knifes back, and I think: shit, he's gonna get whiplash. I position myself on the sofa. Right next to him. I put my arm under his neck, around his shoulder.

I wait.

Chabela and the kid come out of the bathroom.

I say: "It's pizza time!"

Chabela's eyes are swollen, and she's wiped her makeup off, but the kid's face is hard like a little nut.

"We're not hungry," Chabela says. "We just had tea."

"But me and my new friend are ready. How 'bout it?" I give him a big elbow in the side, and he jerks awake.

"*Hey, hey!*" he says, kind of soft, like a question. He's rubbing the back of his neck with his free palm.

Chabela says, "Juvi, *you're the fucking bottom.*"

"Precious chihuahuita," I say. "Sweet little birdie. Kiss kiss." But she goes into the bedroom, slams the door. The kid's lookin' at my new friend like he's some kind of cockroach.

"How 'bout it, kid?" I raise my eyebrows and show the dental work. I am being Very Nice. It's Uncle Juvi.

"OK," she says, too perky. "But no anchovies."

"We're flexible," I say. "Very flexible."

* * *

Chabelita sets up the VHZ, BHS, XYZ what-ever-ya-call-it. She rented *Godfather III,* just like I said. It's in English, but I get the gist. Plus I've seen it four times already.

The pizza takes a while. It comes when the Godfather's Atlantic City meeting is getting ripped up with machine gun fire. That's my favorite part. POW! CH-CH-CH-CH-CH-POW! Chabela's still in the bedroom, packing. Everything in plastic bags. Brush the hair, examine state of collagen injections. Brush the teeth, examine state of bonding job. Curl the eyelashes, fix the makeup. We're sitting on the floor in front of the sofa. It's good, this American pizza, it's always good. Gooey cheese, bell peppers, mushrooms, greasy sausage, thick tomato, onion, lots and lots of onion. I LOVE onion.

I say: "*I invite you to Poland.*"

The kid nods—of course. But of course. We just love going to
Poland, don't we? Our ambassador and his wife are SUCH dear-hearts.
My new friend has a wad of pizza punching out the side of his mouth.
He swallows, and for an instant I panic: this big lump is going down
his throat, he's gonna choke, I don't know nothin' 'bout no Hime-lick
man-oover, get Chabela out of the bathroom, WHAT are we gonna do
with the body, but . . . it's his Adam's apple. Big one!

"*Me?*" he asks. He's looking at the pile of shopping bags in the
corner. Giorgio Armani at Bloomingdale's mostly.

"*You,*" I say.

"*I got AIDS.*" He laughs, that soft laugh again. So sweet. "*They
wouldn't let me in anywhere.*" I just open my eyes at him. Real WIDE.
He says, "*I don't have a passport.*"

I chew my pizza. The kid chews her pizza. We don't bother to ex-
plain that: Travel is not a problem. There is no class but First Class.
For me, there is always a plane. And if I want the ambassador to meet
me, I just call my brother. Guv, I say, I'm going to the North Pole. Tell
my secretary, he says. Whatever you want. Like last month, when
the kid was taking piano lessons. Mozart. Beethoven, you know. Up
and down, up and down, CHORDS. I'm a patient guy. We go to Marrakesh for the weekend, and the Mamounia says the penthouse does
not have a piano. I say there's a piano. They say, mess-sewer, dare
eez no pee-ah-no. I call my brother, he calls his secretary, it goes on a
couple of Platinum cards, and GODDAMMIT there's a fucking PIANO.
An ebony baby grand. Broke open the roof and lowered it down with
a helicopter.

Not a problem.

They forgot the napkins, so I wipe my hands on the sofa. HEY!
Eight hundred bucks a day for this place, like the air is different in
here or something?

* * *

My new friend does have whiplash. But what are Walgreen's braces for? The kid goes out, gets a cab, and picks one up. She brings it back, at the part when Diane Keaton goes to Sicily to hear her son, the opera singer. My friend is crying, but it's a quiet kind of crying. I don't understand his English too good, so I tell Chabelita to ask him what's the matter. He's got pain. OK, I tell Chabelita, put him in the neck brace, get some aspirin. But it's not the neck. It's something else, and he wants percodan. A prescription narcotic.

Percodan? No problem. The problem is clothes. How are we gonna go to Poland, tonight, with no clothes for our new friend here?

I look at Chabelita. Sometimes she's a little slow, but she gets it. Uncle Victor's pee-ed-a-tayre on 74th Street. She knows I know she has the key.

She misses the end of the movie. The Godfather has lived a long and lonely life. He's sitting in his garden, wearing a cardigan sweater. He keels over.

* * *

At ten we go KLM to Warsaw. KLM is better than Lufthansa. Mexicana? U.S. airlines? Why not go Aeroflot? KLM gives you more space, you can lie down, stand up and stretch, walk around. When I push my seat back, all the way, put the foot rest up, my toes don't touch the seat in front of me. OK, I'm short. But you get the picture.

Me and my new friend sit together, Chabela and the kid in the next row. The steward hands us each a hot towel, lemon-scented. Then earphones, and a little blue bag full of stuff. Let's see: a comb, a soap, a razor, mini shaving cream. Jill Sanders aftershave sample, moist towelette, nail file, lotion, mouthwash. Toothbrush, earplugs, eyeshades.

The kid saves these! A couple of months ago, Chabela found a drawerful, maybe twenty little bags, and she told the maid to throw 'em out. Chabelita was so mad she locked herself in her room all day. Wouldn't go to school, wouldn't come down to eat. After supper, I banged on her door, and I yelled, kid, what were you gonna do with all that crap? Pack it up and send it to Mother Teresa?

I know the kid: she's gonna stuff the KLM earphones into the seat pocket in front of her, take out her very own Sony walkman, listen to "Flans" and fool around with her computer. Chabela pushes her seat all the way back. The steward brings her a pillow and two blankets, she puts in her earplugs, pulls down her eyeshades. She looks like something in a cocoon.

Chabela, Chabela. My little sweetie pie. Once she called me *mon petit chou*. I looked it up in the kid's French-Spanish dictionary. You know what it means? It means "my little cabbage." That's disgusting! Cabbage makes you fart like hell. Which is exactly what I'm gonna do. All that ONION, God.

* * *

Soon after takeoff, my friend is using a lot of Kleenex, coughing and hacking and spitting. I'm getting kind of annoyed. I pound him on the back a few times and he looks better. They bring us little dishes of mixed salted nuts and champagne.

"*Hey rad,*" he says, and gulps down the champagne. The steward brings him another. And another. I sip mine slowly. It's not so good. I can't tell what it is, but Dom Perignon it ain't. Maybe I should go Lufthansa. Dinner comes on a linen-covered cart. We start out with cucumber vichyssoise with shellfish butter, then paté of duck with endive and pears. My friend doesn't say anything, just eats with his face over his plate. I push this stuff around with my fork—no room. Then we get little glasses of grapefruit sorbet. He leans back, stiffly with the neck brace, screws up his face.

He says, "*Don't eat the yellow snow!*" Starts laughing like a hyena.

I am eating my sorbet. Cleanses the palate, you know. But I don't get what's this about yellow snow.

"Don't eat the yellow snow," he says again, sputtering from a laugh into a cough. *"My ma used to always say, don't eat the yellow snow."*

I spoon out the last of my sorbet. I look at him, like OK, and so what?

"That's where the dog pissed," he says, flat. My English ain't so good, but I think I get it. There's snow, and where the dog pisses, it's yellow. Well.

He eats the medallions of veal with truffles and baby zucchini. I'm thinking about this, this growing up in the snow. With a dog. There was no snow where I grew up. Dogs lived in the street and ate garbage. I always wondered what snow would be like. I saw rain, and hail, sometimes big round chunks. The Gulf isn't always hot; sometimes the wind blows in, real cold from up north. I imagined snow like crushed hail. I'd seen it in movies, sure. I saw Bing Crosby in *White Christmas,* I saw Jimmy Stewart in *It's a Wonderful Life.* First time I saw snow up close I was twenty-one. I thought it would surprise me, but it didn't. First time I went into a big supermarket, an Aurrerá, I was seventeen. And there was dog food! I couldn't believe it. People actually bought their dogs big bags of special food—Purina—at the supermarket. That was Mexico City.

And in the United States! Lots of snow, lots of dog food.

But I didn't have to work the cane fields three years. My brother was moving up through the ranks, he was in the one and only Party, and assistant to the Chief of Staff of the Minister. I could have called him, asked for a job. I could have started a business. Gotten lots of government contracts, ha! It's so easy. It's just so, so easy. I see that now, how easy everything is. I knew it was easy then too, everyone does, but I thought: not easy for me. I'm just some dumb *naco* from the Gulf, what do I know? What do I have to say? I'm just nobody. I don't know nothin' 'bout nothin'. I was seventeen, I'd finished school, or school had finished me. I got fired from my job—I was a waiter in a café on the plaza. Our ma was dead, a long time, and I didn't know where else to go, so I took the train to Mexico City to see my brother. He was busy. He had to be with the Chief of Staff every minute, and the Chief of Staff had to be with the Minister every minute. Politics.

My brother lived by himself in a big empty house in Las Lomas, but he had a lot of girlfriends. They were tall, with curled hair, big boobs, and they wore high heels, lots of green and blue eyeshadow. He bought 'em gold bracelets and silver earrings at a store called Bustillos de la Fuente. I thought they looked like the transvestites back in Veracruz, the ones that file through the cafés at night, blowing air kisses at the sailors. I remember, the Americans and the Russians used to beat the shit out of 'em. The Germans liked to throw stuff. Napkins. Bits of avocado.

It was the rainy season, and a lot colder up there than around the Gulf. The tiles in the house sucked the heat out of the air, everything was cold. He took me to a restaurant, but the food was strange, no tortillas, too many forks and spoons. Everyone stared at me, my dumb *naco* pants and shirt, borrowed tie and jacket too big.

I jumped on the first bus that left the station. It passed through the south part of the city, then to Tlalpan. It was raining a cold slick kind of rain and the clouds hung real low. We went up the mountains, no sky, just gray, then down to Cuernavaca. It was clear and warm in Cuernavaca, and it seemed like every wall had bougainvillea hanging over it. Orange, red, yellow, white, purple. Palm trees. I pushed down the window and got a faceful of the smell of fresh dirt and sun on wet grass. I started feeling better. The bus went through the town, dropped some people off, then on to Cuautla, a dusty little place, with stops, about half an hour out. The cane fields spread out, swaying in the sun, and men walked along the highway in their huaraches, sombreros, and white pants and shirts. I felt like it, so I got off.

I spent three years working in the cane fields. There isn't much to say about it, 'cept that I liked how I'd get a rhythm going, see the muscles on my arm flex and ripple. Your mind, in this kind of work, is free, free and calm, and you can let it wander, let it consider things, deeply. No one cares about nothin' complicated, like forks and jackets and ties, they just work like dogs, live their lives. Use their woman, get drunk. But there were rats in the fields, and one day I got bit. It gave me some kind of infection, and my leg swole up so bad I had to stay in bed two weeks. And lying there on my crummy little cot, in this dark little adobe hut, I said to myself, Juventino, you are some kind of asshole.

That was a long time ago. Twenty-five years. A lot can happen in twenty-five years.* Now I go anywhere, I do anything. Chabela is a

---

*Translator's note: Three water-damaged sheets of foolscap detailing, in a purportedly autobiographical fashion, Mr. Pérez López's *modus operandi,* or shall we say, *entourloupette,* and *in flagrante dilecto,* were found with Mr. Pérez López's effects, i.e., not *in situ.* The authenticity of this document has been broadly challenged. Nevertheless, *ipso jure,* it is *pari passu* with the main text translated here, consistent with the *allegro ma non troppo* Mr. Pérez López has affected, and most certainly reflective, again, *ipso jure,* of Mr. Pérez López's *Weltanschauung,* and too, let us be blunt, of a certain *Zeitgeist,* a (regrettable) *genius loci;* further, it was written in a similar loopy scrawl with a No. 2 pencil of precisely the width issued by the New York stockbrokerage house where Mr. Pérez López maintained an account from 1976 through February of 1991. Although there is a firm consensus that Mr. Pérez López is not, by any stretch of the imagination, an example of the *evolué,* we must ask ourselves, Do we live in the Land of Goshen? Do we want to live in the Land of Nod? Or do we want to, as the Americans say, Smell the Coffee?

You want to know how I got my money?

WHAT DID YOU THINK?

I'm a BUSINESSMAN. I meet the needs of the market. I buy low, I sell high. I have a number of businesses.

What are they? Well, for example, I have a little nursery. A few greenhouses, couple of trucks, wheelbarrows. I grow flowers, mostly. Daffodils, roses, carnations, and tulips—sunshine yellow. We import the bulbs from Holland. And, at Christmas time, poinsettias. Beautiful

beautiful woman. The kind who expects raspberry chocolate walnut torte. The kind who gets raspberry chocolate walnut torte. Here it comes. I make room.

* * *

I see the kid's overhead light on, like a laser beam down to that laptop thing. I wonder what she's doing with it. I hear her tippity tap tapping, I hear some *beep beeps*. Phaser guns. Then she slams it with her little fist.

Chabela's light is out, has been since we took off. I know she's lying there, all wrapped up, deaf and blind. She's not gonna eat any raspberry chocolate walnut torte. That's how she is. But Chabela fools you. You think she wants to stay inside her cocoon, just like we stay inside this plane—who would pull open the latch? Throw yourself out into the freezing blackness, how high up over the Atlantic?

I saw Chabela's first husband about a month ago. It was a wedding party at the Hacienda Los Morales, one of those things with

---

velvety red and white poinsettias. The Guv believes in civic pride. He makes sure all the public buildings' grounds in all the state have freshly planted flower beds, every three weeks. And you see, I can help him with that.

What else? I have a little paint company. A modest operation. We just produce four colors: white, yellow, red, and green. But those are the only colors you need for highway lines, no parking strips, and stoplight poles. In all the cities and all the towns in all the state. The Guv likes to see fresh paint, once a month.

I also have a little paper factory. Makes stationery, envelopes, that sort of thing. Used in all the offices of all the bureaucracy in all the cities and all the towns in all the state. And big fat rolls of newsprint. The Guv says more paper factories could produce an oversupply of paper. And then we might have unemployment in our state. Which we wouldn't want, no. But my factory does tend to have shortages when the local newspaper columnists are being, you know, less than objective.

I also make investments. 'Specially in real estate. I buy large tracts near where there will be, for example, a new airport. Or a new highway. The Guv always confides in me, you know, his plans for economic development.

I could tell you about my uniform factory, my little garbage collection enterprise, my desalination plant. And my construction company. And so on. But what is there to say, 'cept that I got the MIDAS TOUCH?

a thousand people, men in dinner jackets, the women in something they bought in New York, or the Dallas Galleria. Pink roses and fat white candles on every table, lobster soup and filet mignon. You know, the bride got her dress in La Jolla and the honeymoon's in Hawaii. They're all the same. Chabela was talking to a couple of Victor's friends at another table, and I was just sitting at one of the far tables, working on a cognac and trying to get my cigar lit. The music was givin' me a headache. Must have been something from "Flans." This guy in a long-tailed tuxedo and a black T-shirt, looking like a conductor, or some kind of giant insect, I don't know what, came up and just sat down. Planted his elbows on the table, shoved his face at me. He was stinking drunk. Pedro Armendáriz, Clark Gable, I knew who this guy was.

He said, "You look like Chabela's third husband."

Well. How very reassuring.

He threw a limp arm at me. Wanted me to shake his hand. "Welcome to this very nonexclusive club." Sounded like *fairy noneshooʒiv.* I could tell this was gonna be a problem. I left his hand there, like a dead fish. He flopped it back into his lap.

"She's going to leave you too," he said, leaning forward, like he wanted to stick his nose in the ashtray. "She leaves everybody." He sat back up and ran his fingers through his hair, as if it felt funny. Then he leaned over to one side, very far. His eyes bulged. "Me," he said, "the next guy. You too. Hell, you don't even know who that kid's father is." He started this sick squawking, too shit-faced to laugh, but no one heard it with the music so loud. Then he sang, *"You're the top! You're the top!"* He twirled a napkin around his head, *"You're the This! You're the That!"* He swatted the napkin a little too near my face. *"You're Mickey Mouse!"*

I socked him in the jaw, hard. He fell off the chair and lay flat out on the floor. Then I sat back down, got my cigar lit. Two of the waiters carried him out.*

But what did I see? Chabela sitting there, way across the room, flippin' her hair around at Victor's friends. She's got her little black shantung silk mini hiked up to Harlingen, she's leaning over the table, asking to get her cleaveage examined. I jam my cigar in the cognac. SSSNFT. Courvoisier, my butt. More like Don Pedro, some kind of *naco* shit.

* * *

We do not EXIT the plane with the other passengers. We go out first. It's late morning, and gray, everywhere. The ground, the sky. The customs building. Big murky soup. Herminio and Flor are standing on the tarmac with their Polish driver. They're bundled up in long wool coats, scarves, gloves, big hats with earflaps. Cheeks blotchy pink. They each have a bunch of red roses, wrapped in plastic. One for Chabela, one for Chabelita.

---

*Translator's note: Unbeknownst to Mr. Pérez López, Filiberto Figueroa Paleta and Primitivo Gómez Gómez, Revolutionarily Institutional Waiters' Syndicate (RIWS) members Nos. 213,854 and 327,986, had made the previous acquaintance of the gentleman who was indisposed by Mr. Pérez López at the wedding of Miss Ifigenia Andrade Pechel and Mr. Karl Martínez López (no relation to the narrator whatsoever). According to the December 1990 issue of *Casas y Gente* magazine, lobster soup and filet mignon were in fact served, although Mr. Pérez López neglects to mention an exquisite *sorbet de pamplemousse* and a *paté de canard en croûte*. Said indisposed gentleman, one Pedro Conejo, aka Estaban Rodríguez, had been, *ab inicio*, involved in the so-called "Movement," which culminated some ten days prior to the 1968 Olympic Games. Among other activities, such as handbill printing and distributing, demonstration attending, simplistic slogan shouting, bell-bottom wearing, electric guitar playing (and doing a truly Bad—in the pure, Fussellesque sense—imitation of Jimi Hendrix), and the passing of coin boxes at traffic intersections, Mr. Conejo attempted to organize a waiters' union. Then: Tlatelolco, *Kulturschande à la mexique. (Sui generis?* Hardly: Tien an Men Square; Kwangju; Bloody Sunday; Monthly events in the more remote provinces of northern Bangladesh.) Mr. Conejo and Messrs. Figueroa Paleta and Gómez Gómez were incarcerated (incommunicado, *sans* habeas corpus, *ad lib, ad nauseum*) in Military Camp 1, then transferred to Lecumberri Prison. While Messrs. Figueroa Paleta and Gómez Gómez were not released until 7 January 1984, Mr. Conejo was released on 3 November 1968, requiring only very

I hold up a palm: it's drizzling.

Chabela and the kid go clattering down the steps, and the kid shouts, "Auntie Flor! Uncle!" Course they're not relatives, just act like they are. My friend looks shaky, a little yellow maybe, and he's coughing into his third Kleenex just since he got out of his seat, but he gets down the stairs, right in front of me. He's got Chabela's old black Perry Ellis coat on his arm, and you know, he doesn't look too bad in Victor's Ralph Lauren pinstripe. The back of his neck brace is a dull white, same color as the plane.

Herminio and Flor smile with lots of teeth—I know that kind of smile. It's: SHIT! They're FINALLY here! And I'm bloody fuckin' COLD. Herminio gives me a big clap on the back, Flor pecks me on the cheek. They look at the ground when they shake my friend's hand. Don't ask his name, but they already know it. It's Peter Rainbow. The Guv called Herminio so he'd have the passport ready.

The driver takes our hand luggage. Luis Vuitton, of course. Not that he'd know the difference.

We get into a private bus and head towards the customs building. Rainbow's hacking away into another Kleenex, and Chabelita's got her face in the roses, doesn't want to look up. Herminio sits there with that plastic smile, the buttons across the middle of his coat 'bout to pop off. Flor and Chabela are already on 78 rpm and now Flor

---

minor plastic surgery, mostly to the testicles. Mr. Conejo (who we might think of as a sort of Ur-Sancho Panza) subsequently wrote a series of conciliatory articles for the Sunday edition of *Excélsior,* founded the RIWS, and married the daughter of the Ambassador to the Court of St. James (also granddaughter of the founder of the Banque de Mexique du Nord et Sur et Oueste), the "Chabela" (an Ur-anti-Dulcinea Del Toboso?) Mr. Pérez López so insistently refers to in the text. Once Messrs. Figueroa Paleta and Gómez Gómez had carried Mr. Conejo behind a potted plant and revived him by mopping his brow with a damp towel, they beat the shit out of him. All of which later figured (in a rather circuitous, serendipitous, and indeed essentially numinous fashion) in the tax evasion charges filed against the Governor of the State of Veracruz on 1 March 1991. Messrs. Figueroa Paleta and Gómez Gómez will not be reappearing in this short story; both have taken their annual holiday at the Revolutionarily Institutional Waiters' Syndicate Hotel and Recreation Center (RIWSHRC), which overlooks scenic Los Hornos beach in Acapulco. But I digress.

wants to know how come the kid's not in school. She's so practical, this Flor. Always wants to do everything the nice way, the right way. Her eyes squint up when she looks at me.

"But Chabela," she says in that flowery voice, drives me crazy, "it's February, the middle of the spring term!" I just roll my eyes. What's school? Just a lot of bullshit. Chabela thinks so too, but she humors Flor. Flor's her best friend, from way back, from the little school with the nunnies.

"No, it's not the middle yet, Flor. And Chabelita will only miss a week. There's lots of days 'till June, lots of days." Chabela has a laugh like a wind chime. "And we wanted so much to see you, you and Herminio . . ."

Herminio looks like he has heartburn. And he's going to have to send his driver back, for the diplomatic pouch with the percodan.

We walk right up to passport control. Herminio, Flor, and the driver are waved through, then Chabela and the kid—lots of shuffling and stamping. I step up with mine and Rainbow's passports. Herminio got a photo that's close enough—it's the Polish driver, looking kind of confused.

No problem.

We go through a side building, a private lobby, and then straight to the car. A silver Mercedes. Someone will bring our luggage later.

* * *

In the car, Flor is telling us a lot of stuff we already know. Like she's unhappy. She misses Mexico. Her son, his baby, her mother who's got a bad case of rheumatoid arthritis. Her friends. Chabela's the only one who ever comes to visit. No one here speaks Spanish 'cept for the people from the other Latin embassies. The Mexicans, the Chileans, Argentinians, Venezuelans, and the Cubans, they all stand around at each other's cocktail parties, drinking rum and colas and telling the same old jokes. They're like people stuck in an elevator. By now they hate each other. And one tires, Flor says, of pork and potatoes. And potatoes and pork. Because when you're tired of pork and potatoes, there's potatoes and pork.

But things are a little better than they were last year. The fat guy with the mustache is up for reelection, and the lines outside the stores are gone. The grocery has canned pineapple, and Donald Duck brand orange juice from Greece. But now there's too many Rumanians wandering around. These look like gypsies, with faces the color of river mud. They come into Warsaw by train, and they beg. Watch your purse, Flor says. Especially you, Chabelita. Hold it tight, like this.

* * *

Warsaw in February is gray. Warsaw in July is gray. WARSAW IS FUCKIN' GRAY. And brown, Poles are big on brown. Everything everywhere is peanut-brittle brown, dog-shit brown. Carpets. Bedspreads. Bathroom tiles. And orange. All mixed up in this horrible combination, like those *naco* sweaters they sell at Aurrerá. That's how the Warsaw Inter-Continental looks. Out front there's a huge gray space, some kind of marching ground. And on the other side, way out there, is the ugliest building I ever saw. It's three gigantic concrete shoe boxes, one on top of the other. Gift of Soviet People. Must be! Out to the left, a little park full of trees. But it's winter, so they look like black sticks. People wind their way through, bundled up in coats and hats, walking their dogs. And how's this for a view from the Inter-Continental? Tomb of the Unknown Soldier. One of those serious lookin' white marble things. It's just columns holding up a roof, and in the middle of this thing, in a marble bowl, they got a little fire going. But it's just a flame, for show. Doesn't give off any heat. Two soldiers stand there all day, all night. You know, big coats, rifles, those crummy fake fur hats. Like a couple of Gotta-Get-a-Gund furry donkeys fell on their heads.

Soldiers never move. Some kind of military respect for the dead thing. Military, ha. (Did I do my year of military service? What will a bottle of tequila not buy?) But these guys OBEY. They don't talk, they don't smile, they don't even sneeze. They just sniffle once in a while, and sometimes they sway. You can hardly tell, you have to be real close, but they do, they go heel to toe. Toe to heel. They do.

Three things I like best about Warsaw: the salmon, of course. The Soviet wedding cake building, always makes me laugh. It's the Ministry of Polish Culture. Gift of Soviet People. And third: the whores at the Inter-Continental. They don't walk around outside on the street, uh-huh. Not in this cold. They parade through the lobby, like models. Look at my long blonde hair! At my leatherette miniskirt in dog-shit brown! Their pimps stand over by the magazine rack, scoping the lobby in their black motorcycle jackets.

Herminio's up at the desk with the kid, her face still stuck in the roses. He's checking us in, and I'm sitting here with Flor and Chabela, and Rainbow. Two of the whores are having a parade break, and they sit behind us, smoking cigarettes. Flor's waving her gloves around, complaining about the smoke, complaining about the girls, the corruption of the Inter-Continental management, the corruption in general.

Such a problem, here in Warsaw, here in Poland.

Rainbow's sitting with his back to Flor and Chabela. But I can see he's crying again. Clenching his teeth.

The kid skips up and squeezes in next to Flor. "Mommy," she says, "Mrs. Ceausescu goes to the Louvre, on an official visit!" Flor looks nervous. Herminio's done, he's coming over. Chabela smiles at the kid, keep going, keep going. But the kid has that kitty cat smile. She runs her tongue over her lip.

"They show her around the museum," she says. "Mrs. Ceausescu stops in front of a painting. She says, 'Is this a Matisse?' And the French official sniffs. He says, 'Noh, mah-dahm, eet eez a Renoir.' They see some more paintings. Mrs. Ceausescu stops again. She says, 'Is this a David?' The Frenchman says, 'Noh, mah-dahm, thees eez a Corot.' They stop again. Mrs. Ceausescu says, 'Is this a Picasso?' He says, 'Noh, mah-dahm. Eet eez a mirror.'"

The kid's the only one laughing. Herminio heard the last lines. And now he smiles at me, and he looks like the heartburn went to his face.

* * *

We've unpacked, had coffee. It's late morning and it's the same: gray. But now it's snowing, heavy. Big sloppy blobs. Rainbow's dosed with percodan and we're all in the lobby when Flor comes back to pick up Chabela and the kid, to see the new puppy, she says. Maybe she does have a new puppy, could be. She's got another car, little green thing, looks like a tin can. Tells us the other Mercedes, her Mercedes, got bashed up last week, says someone threw rocks at it. Tires blown out, red spray paint all over the sides. Even with the diplomatic plates! Her voice is high and shaky, like an old lady's.

They get up to go. They put on their coats and their hats. Chabela pecks me on the cheek and the kid sticks her hand up in a sort of half wave.

Yeah, *Sieg Heil* to you too.

Rainbow says he wants to take a walk. Not too far. Over there, he points at the window, to the trees, the other side of the marching ground, to where the little white marble thing is. His face is yellower, and he's working on a new box of Kleenex, filling up his pockets, but I think he's doing better. I'm an optimistic kind of guy.

* * *

We get there, he asks me something. But my English ain't so good. I go, "*What?*" He asks me again. I think he's asking me what is this white marble thing, what is this marble bowl with this eternal flame business, how come it's got two soldiers standing here like statues? I grunt, *Yes*. I don't know how to say this, but I think: What a couple of jerks. Get paid spit and you stand there all day like a piece of furniture in a deep freeze. I mean, this definitely don't beat goat herding.

So I'm thinking: Let's prod. Let's poke. Respect for the fuckin' DEAD. Uh-huh. My German sailor friends taught me a few choice words. Me and Rainbow walk up to these guys, real close. I run my glove over the rim of the marble bowl. The flame is a thin flame— just a lick of orange-colored air. Rainbow pulls the Perry Ellis tighter around the neck brace. One of these Poles has a lumpy nose, the other one has bad skin, all rutted and oily. Rainbow's face looks worse though, his sores are open, fresh.

I say, real loud, "*Dein Gesicht glänzt wie ein Affenarsch!*" Your face shines like an ape's ass.

No reaction. Potato Nose sniffles. Sniff, sniff. They both stare straight ahead. They blink. Blink. Sniff.

I stand right in front of Potato Nose, so close I can smell his wool coat, wet and mothbally. I say, "*Ich pisse dir gleich ans Bein!*" I'd just as soon piss on your leg.

His face reminds me of a noise. A snattling in my glove compartment. They stare out at the marching ground, dead concrete sea. Maybe they don't know German. Maybe it's like Flor says, only the older people know German. But I think they know German. I want to punch one of 'em in the face.

Assholes.

Rainbow's standing there with his mouth hanging open, wheezing. He's stiff. Clenching his fists. I have to hold him up, all the way back to the Inter-Continental. And Oily Face and Potato Nose follow us with their eyes. I can feel them on my back, like X-rays.

* * *

I am bored. There's no videos. There's no shopping, no Broadway shows. The telephones are even worse than in Mexico. It's still too early to call my stockbroker. Rainbow's sleeping, or passed-out, I don't know which. So I'm doing curlicues around the spots on the ceiling with my eyeballs. Every spot tells me a story I already know. I know all there is to know about Rainbow. And what I don't know, I can invent, and it's just the same.

Take this brown one here, looks like a melanoma. He dropped out of high school in Detroit. He had a girlfriend, a nice blonde girl with pink painted nails, but he forgot her birthday 'cause he'd smoked too much pot. Her name was Cindy and she cried and she went to get an ice cream sundae with her best friend. Debbie. At the shopping mall. Or it was New Jersey and her name was Tracy and she didn't shave her armpits. She was fat, wore zodiac rings on every finger, slept with other guys.

The dog, the one that peed in the snow, that one was a collie and it got a skin disease and it ran away. Or it looked just like Benji, from the movies. Sweet little face, nice personality.

SPLAT. Mack truck on the interstate.

Rainbow's father was a janitor in a chemical factory. Or he pumped gas, and he left for a truck-stop waitress with Big Hair when Rainbow was three. His mother was crazy, left him locked in broom closets, no food, no water. He got sent to a foster home. Where they beat him and they fed him baloney sandwiches and fizzy orange drink.

He watched a lot of TV.

When he was seventeen, Rainbow bought a dirty green backpack.

He went to Oaxaca on a bus. When he got there, he got some pey-
ote. He slept on a bench in the plaza, he communed with the people.
The people spit on hippies. YES! It was the shopkeeper with the little
miscelánea at the corner, on his way home after a twelve-hour day. Or
one of the Indian kids selling Chiclets in the cafés. Did it just to see
if he could.

Later, Rainbow went to New York. He worked as a messenger, de-
livering packages on a bicycle. Or maybe he sold pot in Ziploc baggies
in the park. Or washed dishes for a deli. He mainlined heroin, he
smoked crack, zoned out in a tenement somewhere in Harlem. Then
he started selling himself to men, on the street, for a little extra money.

So here we are, one way or another.

* * *

But I don't know what's with Flor. I say the food in Poland is good.
They have smoked fish—trout, and salmon that's firm and pink, not
like what they give you in New York, limp stuff that's been freezing on a Norwegian ship for three weeks. There's duck with baked
apples, goose with raspberry sauce. Cabbage and caraway seeds, lots
of paprika—pickled strip of paprika, could be a Mexican chile. (Note
to self: call the Guv, start import business.) And poppyseed cake,
with slathers of white butter frosting. Top it all off with a cherry
brandy! The restaurant at the Inter-Continental is okay, but sloppy
sometimes, and the waiter always bugs me, tries to sell me Cuban
cigars, 40 dollars a dozen, he whispers, real loud, right in my ear.

The best, the best of the best of the top, that's Wierzynek in
Krakow, 'bout three hours by car.

I make my plan. By three, Rainbow's feeling better. He gets another
percodan and a cup of coffee. The kid's seen the puppy, Chabela and
Flor are talked out—for the morning at least. Herminio's busy, so

we hire a car and driver, and we get to Wierzynek by six. Wine and women, good food and good company.

Smacznego! A sleepy ride back in the snowy night.

* * *

Then Chabela comes back at one, alone. I can't tell her my plan, 'cause she just throws her coat and purse down and says, "Chabelita would not come back with me."

This registers. She's got her hands on her hips, and she looks like a big angry bird. A crow maybe. Her nose twitches. Then she crumples, and she hugs herself and she starts to cry.

What is there to say to this? Chabelita's a pain in the butt. Flor's a bad influence. This can be taken care of. This can be fixed. I pat the bed. Come 'ere, my little sparrow. But she grabs her coat and bag and goes back to the door.

"I have to walk, Juvi. I have to go think. I don't know what to do, how to handle this. I just—"

She's gone.

* * *

I figure she's gonna go out to Old Town and back. That's her favorite walk—a good fifteen minutes out, fifteen minutes back, nice and pretty. Old Town was flattened in the war, but they built it back, exactly like before. Now it looks like Disneyland, Epcot Center. 'Cept there's nothin' to buy, it's cold as hell, full of them Rumanian beggars.

I'm thinking maybe that's what we should do, take the kid to Epcot. She'll have fun, pose with Mickey, go on the rides. Plus it's educational, so that'll shut Flor up.

* * *

I'm not gonna lie here, just lie here on the bed. I'm gonna take a walk too. With my friend Rainbow.

* * *

The sun's out now, but it's too bright and the wind is biting cold. I put on my Bijan sunglasses. Rainbow doesn't have any, so he's squinting, squinting and spitting. Hacking. Wheezing. I gotta pull him out the revolving door by the Perry Ellis. He points to the Tomb of the Unknown Soldier.

Okay, one more time. I'm flexible.

We get there. It's the same. Same, same, SAME. The marble. The little bowl with the little flame. Big gray marching ground. Potato Nose and Oily Face. Fuckin' robots. Rainbow's wheezing. He leans against the wall. It's got some kind of Polish *blah blah blah*, 1945, *blah blah*. He's got that round and watery look in his eyes again.

You know, Chabela says my problem is I gotta be more friendly. Relax. Think about the four-cheese linguini at the Café des Artistes. Loosen up. OK. So I cross my arms. I'm thinkin'. I could make some conversation. Like maybe I could say, Why gentlemen, don't you think, *Sie verkaufen viel Scheissdreck an die Turisten,* They sell a lot of shitty junk to the tourists. In Veracruz they sell stuffed and varnished frogs. They're standing up, nailed to little blocks of wood. They play the marimba, they have little hats glued to their heads. LA BELLA VERACRUZ. Beautiful Veracruz. Uh-huh. But here in Poland they don't sell anything like that. Shawls. Painted eggs. Who cares? Why bother? I mean: ennui. Rainbow's knees buckle. He starts slipping down, and I watch his coat bunch up to his neck brace, I watch those little blonde hairs go down the marble wall, and I see some Polish *blah blah*, I see some more *blah blah*, and Rainbow's just about sitting down on his haunches, like an Indian waiting for the bus. That's when I get mugged. Fat little Rumanian, face the color of river mud.

Rainbow lunges out at him. He gets the scarf, but this guy turns around and pounds Rainbow in the face. ZOCK! In the eye. Rainbow falls on his elbow. But he doesn't cover his eye. He just fingers the scarf and makes a gurgling noise.

Potato Nose and Oily Face. Public fuckin' servants! With rifles! Don't do shit! We're talkin' FURNITURE IN A DEEP FREEZE. What's this bones of the Unknown Soldier? Some asshole stepped on a Nazi mine in 1945? And that Rumanian is across the street and around the block and outta sight. I think I see a bug crawl out from the scarf. My blood boils up to the tiny veins in my eyeballs.

I spit on Potato Nose. Big wad, right on the chest. Forget the German, I give 'em gringo, "*YOU FUCKING FAGGOTS!*"

And Potato Nose sways, heel to toe. Toe to heel.

Oily Face breathes in through his nostrils, real deep. In. Out.

There is no noise, but a distant rumble of bus, a dog barking, somewhere in the naked trees. The wind blows the little flame, and it licks up the side of the bowl, like it wants to get out.

Way out, on the other side of the gray marching ground and the black puddles of slush, I see a turquoise dot. It's Chabela, coming back from Old Town. She's lookin' at the ground, but she's walking over here. One banana, two banana, three banana. Rainbow's still on the ground, and now he's whispering, he's saying "*Scotty! Scotty! Beam me up!*" Whatever that means. But then she sees us. And she turns around. She walks back towards Old Town.

* * *

I open the door to Rainbow's room, and I thought I had him, but I didn't. I drop him and he falls into the room, to the floor. Right in front of the bathroom.

I slam the door shut, and I look down at him. He's not that heavy, but I'm jet-lagged, I'm pissed, I'm huffin' and puffin' from bringing him all the way in from the elevator. I think of Chabela's eyes before she walked out: black, but bright. Not like Josefina's. Like Chabelita's. I think of her back. Turquoise. Reminds me of the sea, but not the Gulf, the Gulf is gray, like hazy blue, muddy green. It was turquoise like the Pacific Ocean, Acapulco, party all day, party all night. And who needs Cole Porter when we got the rumba?

Rainbow's stopped breathing.

I take off my coat, throw it on the chair. Roll up my sleeves. I drag him by the arms over to the bed. Up onto the mattress. A spring pops, a flat *boing*.

I straighten his legs, long in the dark pinstripe. Like the black sticks of trees in the park. I fold the Perry Ellis along his sides. It's damp, spongy from the snow this morning. I rest his hands on his belt.

The backs of his hands are covered with sores, and you can see the bones fan out under the skin, like garden rakes. The edge of his chin is down inside the plastic collar of the neck brace. I look, for a minute, at his face. It looks like it's made of yellow wax. Messed-up yellow wax. His eyes are calm, plain, and empty.

I open the window.

I feel: numb.

But that's 'cause the air is cold. I'm thinking. No kid. No Chabela. No wallet. No Rainbow. Is any of this a surprise? Is any of this REALLY a problem? I suppose it is. Depends on how you look at it. Short run or long run. Long run, no. Short run, yes. I'm gonna have to call Herminio 'bout the body. The Guv, get me some cash. Get a ticket out of this place! Get new plastic, asap.

That means I got the whole day here. Stretching out in front of me like pork and potatoes, and potatoes and pork.

I shut the door, walk out into the hall to go to my room. And two doors down, what do I see? Leatherette Miniskirt in Dog-Shit Brown comes out the door across the hall. Motorcycle Jacket's been waiting outside, and he's not far behind.

I do appreciate certain things.

Motorcycle Jacket says, "*You like?*"

Uh-huh.

"*One hundred dollars.*"

I consider this. Leatherette is twisting her hair. Cute little nose. Skin white and soft and smooth. Long blonde strand. Shiny, flaxy. Pink painted nails.

I say, "*My friend is the one who needs it,*" and I throw open the door to Rainbow's room.